Jennifer Chan

IS NOT
ALONE

Also by Tae Keller

The Science of Breakable Things

When You Trap a Tiger

Jennifer Chan
IS NOT
ALONE

TAE KELLER

Random House New York

Text copyright © 2022 by Tae Keller
Jacket art copyright © 2022 by Dion MBD

All rights reserved. Published in the United States by Random House Children's Books, a division of Penguin Random House LLC, New York.

Random House and the colophon are registered trademarks of Penguin Random House LLC.

Visit us on the Web! rhcbooks.com

Educators and librarians, for a variety of teaching tools, visit us at RHTeachersLibrarians.com

Library of Congress Cataloging-in-Publication Data is available upon request.
ISBN 978-0-593-31052-6 (trade)—ISBN 978-0-593-31053-3 (lib. bdg.)—
ISBN 978-0-593-31054-0 (ebook)—ISBN 978-0-593-56744-9 (int'l)

The text of this book is set in 11.5-point Sabon MT Pro.
Interior design by Cathy Bobak

Printed in the United States of America
10 9 8 7 6 5 4 3 2 1
First Edition

33614082867127

For the girl I was at twelve—
a book fifteen years in the making

Now

The end of everything starts with a buzz. You know the one—the insecty buzz that makes your heart beat faster, that tells you somebody wants your attention.

So maybe I should say: the end of everything starts with a text.

But we'll get to that in a minute. Because right now I'm here, sitting between Tess and Reagan in our school's chapel, my thighs sweat-slipping against the wooden seat, shirt sticking to my back. The overhead fans are spinning, but they're not nearly enough for the small-town Florida heat, even in October.

Reagan fans herself with the concert program and mimes falling asleep. She even lets out a quiet fake snore.

Tess muffles her laugh, and I make wide eyes at them— eyes that say *Pay attention or we'll get in trouble!* but also *You are so right. I'm bored out of my mind.*

I can say a lot without saying a word, which comes in handy during these evening orchestra concerts.

And let's be honest: Reagan can be a bit dramatic, but she's not entirely wrong. We come to these concerts because Tess's sister is in the orchestra, and we can't make Tess attend alone. But the problem with the Gibbons Academy middle school orchestra is that instead of learning new music, they play the same Christmas carols all year, every year. By the millionth rendition of "Silent Night," it's kind of . . . a lot.

Secretly, though, I think there's something comforting about the strings and the familiarity. And today, especially, I welcome the sameness.

Today I'm locked in a battle with my brain, thinking about the Incident from Friday while also *reallynotthinkingaboutit.* My mind keeps drifting, floating to that feeling of my whole self coming apart. And then I have to drag my thoughts right back to this very normal, very boring evening. *See, "Silent Night." Just like it always is.*

And that's when Reagan's phone buzzes.

The text that ends everything.

But I don't know yet that it's an end-everything text. The orchestra begins "Hark! the Herald Angels Sing," and I watch Reagan pull her phone out of her pocket.

For a split second, she frowns at the name on the screen. Then she rearranges her face, like she realized her reaction was wrong. She smiles and raises her brows until they disappear beneath her dark brown bangs. Her blue eyes spark. These are the kind of eyes that say *I have a secret.*

"It's Pete," she mouths.

With a rush of relief, I send a thank-you up to the universe.

This is the perfect distraction. Unlike the Incident, Reagan's drama with Pete is predictable and constant. It's as familiar as a Christmas carol.

"Seriously?" Tess whispers too loudly.

From the pew in front of us, a random dad shushes her, and Reagan rolls her eyes before dropping her gaze to Pete's text.

As she reads, her shoulders stiffen. She doesn't say anything. She doesn't move. But her eyes flick back and forth over the screen, like she's reading the text again and again. I try to look over her shoulder, but she tilts the screen away from me.

Too late, I realize my mistake. That tiny movement, that flick of a hidden screen, signals to Tess that this might be a particularly interesting flavor of gossip—and now she'll never let it go.

"What's it say?" she asks. "Like, you have to tell us?"

Something to know about Tess: every sentence that leaves her mouth is a question. Even when she's making a statement, she ends it with a question mark.

She leans over me to get closer to Reagan, and I try to nudge her away. Tess is all long legs, long arms, tall and thin and sharp. Right now her elbow digs into my stomach, and her red-orange curls stick to my lip gloss. "Tess," I say. "Stop."

I'm distracted, so it takes me a moment to notice Reagan's reaction. She sucks on her lips, and her skin goes so pale that the freckles sprinkled across her cheeks look like bright, bold specks of paint. This is an expression I've seen only once before. Only one time, in over a year of best friendship.

Reagan is scared.

3

My heartbeat leaps into my ears, and I tell it to stop being so dramatic. "Maybe you should put the phone away," I tell Reagan. I can't deny that I'm curious, but after last week, I'm not in the mood for anything intense.

"Um, maybe *don't* put your phone away?" Tess says. "Because you have to tell us what's going on?"

The dad turns to shush us for a second time, but Reagan ignores everyone.

She taps back and forth and back and forth with Pete, until finally she looks up. "There are police cars outside Jennifer's house," she whispers.

Definitely not normal.

"No," I say. At least, I think I say it. Because I *hear* myself speak, but I don't actually register saying the word. I grasp for reasonable explanations. "Do you think the police were just . . . stopping by? Or maybe . . . do you think—"

"Jennifer told the police what we did?" Tess interrupts. "Like, are they coming for us?"

I wish Tess would give this a minute. I wish she would wait one second before jumping to conclusions. I can't process.

My right leg starts shaking, and my heart beats so loud I can't even—

But no, no. This doesn't make sense. We can't go to *jail* for the Incident. I mean, it wasn't great. It's not my favorite thing to think about. But it wasn't that bad. It wasn't *illegal*.

"Don't be stupid," Reagan says, and I can't help but flinch at the way she says the word, her consonants hard and harsh. *Stu-pid*. "The police aren't there for us."

"So, what's—?" Tess starts, but Reagan's phone buzzes again.

She stares at the screen as she whispers to us, "Pete's not supposed to know this, but he heard it from his dad." Pete's dad is the county sheriff, so Pete's always finding out more than he should know.

Reagan swallows. "Jennifer's missing."

I let the words settle over me, thick and icy. The heat and humidity can't touch me anymore. "She's missing," I repeat.

I try to make sense of this, but it's all so weird. Nothing ever happens in this town. Nothing ever happens in Nowhereville.

Reagan looks at me, and beneath the stone in her expression, there's a desperation only I can see. Her eyes say, *I need you*. "Jennifer left a note that said she's, like, running away."

"She ran away." I'm only capable of repeating Reagan's words, apparently.

Leaning over, Tess asks, "Did she say *why*?"

Reagan blinks, like she forgot Tess was there, but I have to admit, I'm glad Tess asked the question. I need to know, too.

Reagan shakes her head. "Not sure. Pete's dad wouldn't show him the note."

Maybe it's not fair, but suddenly I am red-hot mad at Pete. I hate him, seriously. Why would he tell Reagan something like this if he didn't know the whole story? Why would he tell her without that *crucial bit of information*?

"Oh my gosh," Tess says. "Do you think this is, like, Jennifer's revenge?"

The thought makes me woozy.

"Like, do you think Jennifer's trying to get back at us?" Tess pushes. "Trying to get us in trouble?"

Her questions bulldoze any last shred of calm, any scrap of normalcy. I feel like my intestines are disintegrating.

The energy in the chapel shifts, and I notice the whispers. It's almost like Jennifer's news is a physical thing. I can see it moving through the chapel: We find out first. Then Kyle—Pete's best friend—checks his phone and whispers to one of his friends.

Kyle texts someone, and then his girlfriend-of-two-days gets a *ping* and gasps, and then all the sports girls are whispering.

I watch the news ripple through the students. Not all of us are here this evening, but enough. Before the end of the night, nearly everyone will know.

The news moves in waves of popularity through the pews, with some kids turning back to Reagan and me, almost like they want to know how to act. Under their gaze, I feel itchy, shaky, like I have no control of my body.

Too quickly, the news reaches the parents, and they murmur among themselves.

News spreads fast in Nowhereville. That is something to know.

I hear her name, whispered softly at first, then loudly. *Jennifer, Jennifer, Jen-ni-FER.* She's impossible to escape. She's everywhere.

She's not here.

A parent runs up and says something to the conductor, who cuts the music. Phones ring. People talk.

The whole world is too loud.

And I hear it, over and over: "Jennifer Chan ran away. Jennifer Chan is *missing.*"

The end of everything starts quietly, with a buzz you can barely hear. But it doesn't end that way—not even close.

2

The orchestra concert falls apart pretty darn fast after
that.

Everybody starts moving at once, and Tess's mom hurries
over to us. "Oh, what awful news," she says, placing a hand on
Tess's shoulder. Tess's mom is the kind of person who seems
to have a loud opinion and a big reaction to everything, but
tonight her reaction doesn't seem quite big enough. "Let's get
you and your sister home."

"But my friends need me," Tess protests, eyes lit with fear,
confusion, and also, a terrible kind of excitement.

Honestly, it's a relief when Tess's mom tugs her away and
they disappear into a mass of people—a jumble of panic,
questions, suggestions, hands clasped to mouths, and palms
pressed against hearts.

I turn to Reagan. "What are we going to do?"

Reagan shakes her head. Checks her phone again. But
there's nothing from Pete—no text that magically explains
everything.

"You're still sleeping over, right?" I can hear the twinge of desperation in my voice, but for once, I don't bother to stifle it. Violins scream in my head. The world blurs at the edges.

Reagan's brows pinch. "Mal. It's all right. It's gonna be okay."

Right. It's gonna be okay. Just a silent night. Just like any other night.

Mom appears from out of nowhere.

No. That's not true. Not out of nowhere.

Mom appears from her seat in the back of the chapel and wraps her arm around my waist, guiding me away from my friend. "You need fresh air," she says into my ear.

"Wait," I say. "I need Reagan."

Because I'm looking around and suddenly: *Reagan is missing!*

But no. That's not right, either. She's standing right where I left her, frowning at her phone.

My brain isn't working very well in this moment.

Mom leads me through the chaotic crowd and into a quiet corner. Then she kneels in front of me and holds my face in her hands. "How are you doing? Are you feeling faint?"

I close my eyes until the spots stop dancing behind my lids. "I only fainted that one time," I tell her. "It's not, like, a thing."

Mom frowns. There's clearly something she wants to say, but the parent who shushed us earlier walks over and touches Mom's arm.

"Some of us are putting together a search party," he says. "And we need as many people as possible."

I see stars.

"Give us a minute," Mom responds. When he leaves, she repeats her *Worried About Mal* mantra: "Deep breaths. Deep breaths, Mallory."

"I can't . . . ," I start to say. I can't get my thoughts together. Questions pop into my head and then disappear before I can gather them: *Why did Jennifer run away? Where did she go? Did she tell anybody what we did?*

Mom holds my wrist so tightly that I can feel my pulse beating against her thumb. "Oh, honey. I know how scary this is. I know, I know."

"Where's Reagan?" I lost sight of her in the chapel, and she didn't follow us through the crowd.

Mom pulls back. "You don't need to worry about Reagan. She's fine. Tess's parents are taking her home. I know—I know you're worried about Jennifer, but you don't need to worry about Reagan right now."

"They're taking her home? But she was supposed to sleep over."

I know I sound ridiculous, but Reagan has that best-friend way of reaching into my brain and knowing what I'm thinking—even before I do. All I want is to stay up late with her, talking and talking and re-talking about what just happened.

Mom's patience slips. "Mallory, Reagan is *fine*." She takes a breath. *Deep breaths. Deep breaths, Mom.* "I know this is scary. I know you're worried about your friend."

At first, I think she means Reagan, but no. Of course she means Jennifer. *My friend.*

Those words make the world spin. For a second, I'm back in that bathroom again, the one just beneath my feet, in the basement of this chapel, and I'm reliving the Incident. Reagan's words echo in my memory: *Who do you think you are?*

Then I shake my head, snap back, and I'm in the chapel again.

Jennifer Chan ran away.

What kind of person *runs away?*

"I'm right here, honey," Mom says, squeezing my arm. Mom is philosophically opposed to lying to me, so she does not say: *Everything is gonna be okay.*

I glance over her shoulder at the group of my neighbors and teachers—the search party. A search party in Nowhereville, where it's impossible to hide.

And I realize that I'm afraid of what they might find. I'm afraid for Jennifer, for Reagan, for myself. Afraid up to Jupiter and back.

I want to bury myself in Mom's arms, feel her squeeze me tight and hold me. But I'm still at school and I'm surrounded by my classmates, so I just close my eyes and focus on her hand against my arm.

When I speak, my voice doesn't sound like my own. It sounds a little like Reagan's did—halfway between a whisper and a sob. "Is she going to come back?"

Mom doesn't lie. She brushes her thumb against my arm and says, "I don't know."

Then

3

If a buzz is the end of everything, then a pie is the beginning. Because the morning Jennifer Chan moved to Nowhereville, Mom made a pie.

Here's something to know: Mom baking is always a bad sign. When Mom's holding baked goods, she might as well have a blinking sign over her head that says: APPROACH WITH CAUTION.

Mom was facing away from me as I walked into the kitchen, and as soon as I saw the pie, I turned right back around—but Dad looked up and caught me.

"Morning, Mallory," he said, sitting at the kitchen table and sipping what was probably his third cup of coffee. "How'd you sleep?"

I stepped into the kitchen with careful, quiet feet, like I was approaching a sugar-dusted wildebeest. "I slept good."

Mom brushed flour from her hands and turned to look at me. "*Well*, Mallory. You slept *well*." Then she frowned. "What's on your face?"

I shifted. Earlier in the summer, before Reagan left to spend a month in Philadelphia with her twenty-two-year-old sister, Kate, Reagan had started wearing makeup. As a gift, she'd given me her extra eyeliner pencil.

It's not like I wore a lot. Just a little bit under my bottom lashes, to make my plain brown eyes look bigger. With Reagan, it made me feel cool, like I could pass for fourteen instead of twelve.

But Mom made me feel like a kid playing dress-up. Suddenly my eyes stung with almost tears. That was happening a lot with Mom lately.

Dad said, in his typical Dad-language, "She's exploring an outward expression of her inner feelings." Which made me feel worse. It wasn't an outward expression of anything. It was just *makeup*.

Mom shot Dad a look that said *We'll discuss this later*, then cleared her throat. "Anyway, I'm glad you're up. I was just about to welcome our new neighbors to Norwell."

"Oh my god," I said. "You're gonna meet *Jennifer Chan*?" Kind of embarrassing, but my voice dropped to a whisper as I said her name. I couldn't help it. After all the rumors, she was practically a celebrity.

Mom frowned. "And her mother, yes. You may join me."

The news kept getting better and better. "You mean I'd be the first kid in Nowhereville to meet her?"

Dad took a sip of coffee to hide a smile. "Try not to call our town Nowhereville in public, Mal. It's a tad dreary."

Just like that, the weirdness from the makeup conversation

evaporated. Because this was cool. I could confirm the rumors *firsthand*. I had to text Reagan. She'd be so jealous.

When my across-the-street neighbor old Ms. Martin died (R.I.P.), we started watching, waiting to see who would fill the house next. Nobody new had moved to town since Reagan and her dad, and all us kids were hoping to meet someone our age, someone to add just the right amount of interest.

As it turned out, my grade got lucky again, because first came Reagan, and then came Jennifer Chan.

And, wow, the rumors started fast. Before she'd even moved in, we heard stories:

Jennifer Chan karate-chopped some kid at her old school, put him in a full-body cast.

Jennifer Chan moved to Nowhereville to escape juvie.

Jennifer Chan's mom is actually a wanted murderer, and they both had to assume secret identities.

Jennifer Chan isn't even Jennifer Chan's real name!

In Nowhereville, someone's always saying something, and nobody knows what's real. But the truth doesn't always matter. Sometimes the idea of someone, the things people say about them, matters so much more. Because when you think about it, isn't that who we really are—a collection of the things people think about us?

"Apparently she karate-chopped someone and put him in a full-body cast," I told my parents.

Dad snorted into his coffee, but Mom thudded the pie on the kitchen counter. I tried to ignore the scent wafting off it—cinnamon apple, my favorite. "That is a ridiculous rumor," she said, raising a finger at me, "and you know it."

"I'm just saying," I murmured, glancing at Dad for help. He just raised his brows like *You brought this on yourself.*

Lately every conversation with Mom turned into a fight or a lecture, like she didn't trust me to be a decent person on my own.

Mom continued, her voice getting high and sharp. "I just find it very *interesting* that the rumor has to do with this poor girl 'karate-chopping' someone." For some reason, Mom never properly learned how to do air quotes, so she always did them with one finger. We used to joke about it as a family, but not anymore.

"Yeah, Mom. I know. I get it. It's just that . . ." But how could I explain the rumors to her? Nobody was trying to be *mean*. We were just curious.

"That is a racist stereotype, Mallory, and I hope you take a stand against it."

"But, Mom, she really *does* do karate. Reagan and I Googled her."

Mom sniffed, and I knew instantly that I'd said the wrong thing. Mom's half-Korean, and her life's dream was to be an Asian American studies professor and activist, but when Dad got hired as a philosophy professor at Florida Southern College, Mom took a job in its admissions office. The college doesn't have an Asian American studies department.

"Well, *regardless*," Mom said, as if she'd proven her point. She picked up the pie and stood a little straighter. "Let's meet our new neighbors. I want you to be kind and inviting, Mallory."

I tried to say *I am,* but the words wouldn't come out. What was the point, anyway, when she'd already made up her mind about me? When somewhere along the way, she'd decided that I *wasn't* kind and inviting?

I swallowed, following her out the door and across the street. It didn't matter what Mom thought of me. I'd still have a good story to tell at school.

I would still be the first seventh grader to meet Jennifer Chan.

It took Ms. Chan forever to come to the front door. Mom and I stood, smothered by heat and the static hum of cicadas, listening to the crash and clatter of pots and pans and the frantic "Coming! Just a sec!" behind the door.

When Ms. Chan finally threw the door open, she leaned against the frame, trying to catch her breath as strands of hair fell loose from her bun.

Either she'd been busy unpacking or she'd been murdering a new victim. The truth was anybody's guess.

Mom put on an extra-big smile and said, "Hello! Welcome to the neighborhood!"

I did a double take, just to make sure my mother hadn't been body-snatched while I wasn't looking. This was the same person who'd been judging my makeup, just ten minutes earlier.

"Oh, hi," Ms. Chan said, pushing her messy black hair out of her face.

She was younger than most moms, and everything about her screamed *different*—she was so . . . not-Nowhere, with her red-and-yellow-patterned dress, bright orange lipstick (smudged a bit on her cheek), long fake eyelashes, and pan-icked smile that made her look a little lost.

"You must be Rebecca Chan! I'm Leah Moss," Mom said, holding out the pie, "and this is my daughter, Mallory. Mallory is the same age as Jennifer!"

For a few awkward seconds, Ms. Chan blinked at the dessert, like she thought the pie might be Mom's twelve-year-old daughter. Then she looked at me and said, "Oh, right."

Mom smiled and tilted her head. I knew this expression, all warm and nurturing. She got this way with people she wanted to guide and comfort.

She didn't look at me that way anymore.

"Norwell can be—well, all new places can be a bit in-timidating at first," Mom said. "So I thought it might be nice for Jennifer to meet someone her age. You know, to have a friendly face around here."

I smiled, trying to make my face appear as friendly as possible. I was regretting the eyeliner. Did friendly faces out-wardly express their emotions through under-eye makeup?

Ms. Chan looked relieved. "Right, yes. That makes sense. Does Mallory go to Gibbons? I just enrolled Jennifer."

I nodded. There were two schools nearby, Norwell Public School and Gibbons Academy. Ours was the smaller one, so I'd been trying not to get my hopes up. But this. This was exciting. A new kid.

Ms. Chan half smiled and called into the house, "Love-bug! Someone wants to meet you!"

I cringed, partly at the awkwardness of hearing such a

cutesy term, but mostly because in Florida, a lovebug wasn't a cute nickname. It was what we called the bugs that spontaneously descended in May and September to swarm the air and stick to windshields.

I slid a questioning glance at Mom. *Should we tell them?*

Mom grimaced like, *Why is our state like this?* Then she gave the slightest shake of her head. *Probably best not to.*

Jennifer came pounding down the stairs and arrived at the front door, her hair slipping out of a lopsided ponytail. She was basically a younger, rounder version of her mother. And she wasn't wearing eyeliner.

"Um . . . ," Ms. Chan said, looking to Mom for help.

Mom leaned over to talk to Jennifer, resting her hands on her knees as if she were speaking to a kindergartner. "Hi, Jennifer, I'm Leah Moss, and this is Mallory. Mallory is here to welcome you to Norwell and teach you everything you need to know about Gibbons Academy."

Jennifer beamed. "Pleased to meet you!"

Then she looked me up and down, and the dizzy, unpleasant rush of being *watched* smacked into me. I wasn't prepared for that. I'd expected to gain new-kid intel for my friends. I wasn't ready for *her* to judge *me*.

I wondered what she was thinking, what kind of person she was seeing. My stomach twisted.

"I've gone to Gibbons since kindergarten," I said, as if that were relevant information.

Jennifer tilted her head, observing me, and I felt myself holding my breath.

Then she smiled and said, "Come see my new room." Not a question. A command.

I got the intense urge to text Reagan, to tell her what was happening, to ask her what I should do, and I fumbled for my phone in my pocket, feeling the warm, flat surface against my palm. But I didn't dare take it out. Mom would have thrown a fit.

"Mallory would love that," Mom said, placing one hand on my back and guiding me inside. She gestured to the pie and said to Ms. Chan, "Maybe there's somewhere we can put this down?"

Mom was moving us around like little dolls, telling us where to go, and when she and Ms. Chan disappeared into the kitchen, Jennifer led me through the house.

The weird thing about our neighborhood was that all the houses almost looked the same—painted brick facades and big windows, small houses on big lawns filled with oak trees and flower boxes. And from the inside, Jennifer's house was a mirror version of my own, so it was like I'd already been there a million times, except everything was backward— a parallel-universe version of my home.

But instead of using the downstairs bedroom like me, Jennifer had claimed the upstairs one—the one Dad used for his office.

As we climbed the stairs to her room, Jennifer glanced back and gave me a knowing smile, as if we were in some kind of secret club. "So, what kind of Asian are you?"

"Oh." I felt my cheeks flush, though I wasn't sure why. "My mom's half-Korean."

Jennifer crinkled her brow, like I'd said something strange. But she just responded, "I'm Chinese. There aren't a lot of us here, are there?"

"I guess not." We fell back into silence, and I stumbled around, searching for more conversation. "Um, where'd you move from?"

I already knew from the Googling: Chicago.

"Chicago," Jennifer said, taking the stairs two at a time. "Well—Columbus, then Chicago. Now here."

"Oh, cool." When Reagan and I had found out Jennifer was from Chicago, Reagan was annoyed. Reagan had lived in Philadelphia before she moved here—which was way awesome—but Chicago was even more glamorous. "Why did you move here?" I asked.

Jennifer opened the door to her bedroom and, with a sweep of her hand, revealed a bare mattress, a desk, and some boxes. "Here it is. I'm still moving in, obviously."

I wondered if she'd heard my question, or if I should ask again. Sometimes I accidentally spoke too quietly for people to hear. Reagan always pointed that out, gently reminding me to be louder so people would take me more seriously.

"Um, that's cool," I repeated. "So, why—"

"I'll give you the tour," Jennifer interrupted, walking through the maze of her room and pointing at the cardboard boxes. "Clothes: boring. Shoes: meh. Books, coats—ah, here we go!" She stopped in front of a box labeled *INVESTIGA-TION* and waved me over.

I stepped toward her, careful to avoid the piles of clothes she'd started to unpack.

"So, this box is . . ." She looked at me and did that up-and-down judging again. "Have you ever had something strange happen to you? Something you can't explain?"

My palms went clammy. The thing about rumors is that nobody ever believes them. That is, nobody ever believes them *completely* until the person says or does something unusual. Or creepy. Or just plain weird, and then you think, *Well, who knows? Maybe.*

And so in that room, with Jennifer acting all weird, I thought, *She really could karate-chop me. I don't know.*

"I'm not talking about experiencing anything, you know, *wild*," she continued. "I wouldn't expect that from an everyday citizen."

"Right." I took a step back because, um, was she *not* an everyday citizen? Maybe she really was a trained assassin.

"Wait, no, stop," she blurted, holding up her hands. She squeezed her eyes shut and took a deep breath before opening them again. "Ugh, Rebecca told me not to bring this up. Not everyone gets it."

Was calling your mom by her first name something a trained assassin might do? Maybe.

"Sometimes people experience the big things," Jennifer went on, "like lights in the sky—a red flashing three times— or strange messages on the radio. But a lot of times the signs are smaller. Like when you feel a chill in the air, or you get déjà vu, or you wake up from a dream but your body's still asleep and you can't move for a few seconds."

She waved her arms in big circles, gesturing fast, speaking

22

faster. "Or sometimes it's just this feeling you get. Like you want to do or say something, but your body won't let you. Or you feel so lost, like you don't belong, like everyone around you knew there'd be a test, but you didn't, so you didn't study. You didn't even read the *book*."

"Oh."

"And have you ever wondered what those feelings mean?"

My parents were always going on about *intellectual curiosity* (mostly how they wished I had more of it). But, seriously, Jennifer had some major intellectual curiosity.

The truth was, I'd never wondered about any of that. Yes, I got those feelings, but that was just the way things were. There was no use questioning it.

"You probably think I'm a walnut," she said, looking down and nudging the box with her toe.

I could tell she wanted me to like her. She wanted me to like her so badly that it practically radiated off her. You weren't supposed to *try* so hard. You weren't supposed to want things so badly.

And that was when I knew the rumors were false. Because this girl could never survive the world of trained assassins. She'd barely survive Gibbons Academy.

"I don't think you're a . . . walnut," I said.

She let out a big *whoosh* of air, not even bothering to hide her relief, and to my surprise, I realized I wanted her to like me, too.

"But, uh, what do those things mean?" I asked.

She looked at me with hope in her eyes, and her smile

grew, almost like she couldn't stop it, or didn't want to. She whispered, *"Aliens."*

I blinked, waiting for her to say *KIDDING*. But she just stood there, and with every second of silence, every second I stared without saying a word, a tiny bit of that hope slid off her face.

"Oh," I made myself say. It was officially, 100 percent confirmed: the kids at Gibbons would eat her alive.

And in that awful, hope-slipping silence, I knew my friends wouldn't like her. Which meant being friends with Jennifer would be . . . messy. Being friends would be hard for both of us, and sometimes the difficulty wasn't worth it. Even though that thought made me sadder than I wanted to admit, sometimes it was better not to try.

"Actually, I think I have to g—" I began, but she sucked her lips together, like she was swallowing back her disappointment, and something pinched in my chest. I knew I should escape her orbit, but I couldn't get the words out.

In my head, I said, *I have to go.*

But what came out was "What do you mean, aliens?"

Her face lit with relief. "Really? You really want to know? Oh my god, that's awesome. Because there's actually tons of evidence of extraterrestrial life."

From Reagan, I knew confidence was contagious. But with Jennifer, I realized that relief was, too. A tiny knot released in my chest, and the feeling made me giddy. It made me . . . intellectually curious or something. Pointing to the *INVESTIGATION* box, I asked, "Is that what's in there? Evidence?"

"Oh, yeah. It's full of everything I know." She dropped to her knees and ripped the tape off, then lifted the cardboard flaps to reveal sparkling rocks in glass cases, weathered newspaper clippings, and a thick stack of colorful composition notebooks. "And everything my dad knew, too. We used to watch space documentaries and sci-fi movies, and we went stargazing a lot before he died."

"Oh." We weren't close enough for me to comfort her, but I couldn't *not* comfort her. "I'm sorry about your dad," I said, meaning it.

She blinked quickly. Her smile faltered. But then she shook her head and jumped to her feet. "My latest book is in my bag downstairs. I'll show it to you. Wait here!"

She ran out the door and thundered down the stairs, and I stood in that room full of boxes, trying to figure out what to do.

I texted Reagan: I just met the new girl?!

Lightning fast, Reagan responded, Umm?? Jennifer Chan? Did she spring up on you like a ninja??

I started typing, trying not to think about what Mom would say in response. You'll never believe it. She actually believes in—

I stared at the words, at the send button right next to them. From downstairs, I heard Jennifer saying something to her mom, her tone light and fluffy, though I couldn't make out the words.

Slowly, I deleted my text.

Reagan was my best friend in the whole world. She understood me better than anybody—better than my parents, better than Tess, better than any friend I'd ever had. But still. Maybe it was best if Reagan didn't know about Jennifer's aliens.

When I didn't respond, Reagan texted, Um hello?

And then: What was she like? Like Kath and Ingrid level weird, or worse?

I bit my lip. Ingrid Stone and Kath Abrams were unpopular at school, but I still felt awkward whenever Reagan mentioned them. I used to hang out with Ingrid—not a lot, but a little. And then last year, Ingrid started to hate me. I didn't know why, but sometimes, secretly, I wondered if she was jealous that I got popular.

Another text from Reagan: Gory details, please with a pretty cherry??

Jennifer returned and I slid my phone back into my pocket. Reagan would be upset about the cliffhanger, but I wasn't sure how to respond. I didn't want to lie to her—but I didn't want to be totally honest, either.

"This is my current book," Jennifer said, holding up a green composition notebook. On the cover, in big, bold letters that spilled out of the title box, she'd written: *JENNIFER CHAN'S GUIDE TO THE UNIVERSE, VOLUME VII.* "I've been compiling proof, theories, and advice. Obviously, there's a lot of bogus information out there, but that's why you have to educate yourself, so you know what to believe."

I stared at the notebook before meeting her eyes. "So you mean—you really believe . . . in aliens?" I didn't want to sound rude, but it was a valid question.

She smiled, like she'd been expecting the skepticism. "Of course. It might sound wild at first, but there's no way we're the only sentient life-forms in the universe. Think about it. The beginning of everything started with a *BANG*."

I jumped and she laughed before continuing. "And then what? The universe ends with us? With a bunch of humans destroying one little planet? Not a chance. There *has* to be more." She handed me the notebook. "This will help you understand."

"You're . . . giving this to me?" I ran my finger along the bloated, weathered pages. I couldn't imagine filling seven notebooks with . . . anything, and I felt equal parts panicked and touched by her trust.

"I'm *sharing* it. And when you're done reading, I can teach you about *the hunt*."

I hesitated. Something about the way she said it sounded ominous.

"Oh, don't worry. It's not scary. Really, it's all about communication. Aliens are out there. They've *been* out there, ready and waiting, and all we have to do is get in touch. It's just like knowing the right phone number to dial."

"That makes sense," I said. It did, in a kind-of-not-really way.

Jennifer glanced around, as if an alien might be hiding in one of her boxes. She leaned forward. "Can I trust you?"

Without thinking, I nodded.

"Okay, well. I think I know the right phone number. I think I know how to make contact."

I found myself leaning in, whispering, too. "Is that really possible?"

"It could be! And just in time, too. I mean, look at our planet: Huge hurricanes. Raging fires. Pandemics. Half this state is gonna be underwater soon. But if there was someone out there who could help—who could fix our problems or take us somewhere safe, somewhere *new* . . ."

"That would change everything," I finished, getting caught up in her excitement. She was contagious.

"Exactly. And I'll be the first human to make contact. Most people run from the truth. But I run toward it. I'm going to make history. I'm going to change the world."

"I can tell." I smiled without meaning to. I knew I should think she was, well, a walnut. But the thing was, she sounded so confident that I believed her. Not about the *alien* part, maybe—but about making history. I don't think I'd ever heard anybody sound so sure of themselves—not even Reagan.

"See, you're a person who isn't afraid to believe." Jennifer's grin grew wider. "I knew I could trust you."

Jennifer Chan's Guide to the Universe
Volume IV, Entry No. 11: How to Find Your Alien-Hunting Allies

Mom says not to tell anyone about the alien investigation. Or, as she calls it, "alien nonsense."

But Mom is afraid to believe. Mom worries about whether my clothes are wrinkled or my hair is brushed or my thoughts are messy. She's scared of what people will think.

But I call that "people nonsense."

Dad, on the other hand, isn't afraid of people, and he isn't afraid of aliens.

A couple years ago, he told me about a scientific theory called the altruism theory. Basically, a bunch of really smart scientists believe that if an alien civilization becomes advanced enough to travel through space, that means they've already lived through all the bad stuff. They've lived through nuclear weapons and wars and climate change, and they managed not to destroy themselves and their planet.

If they've lived that long, the only way they could have survived is by learning to be good.

So that's why we shouldn't fear them. And I don't think we should fear each other, either. Because even if people haven't quite figured it out, they're learning.

At least, that's what I've always assumed.

But today Dad said something I didn't really understand. We were sitting together in the hospital before one of his treatments, and he said, "You'll need some new allies after I'm gone."

I told him I wouldn't, that I didn't need anyone else, but he just took my hand in his.

"Being brave means going up to people and saying, 'Here's what I believe. I trust you,'" he said. "Trust is the scariest thing to give, but it's the most powerful."

That didn't make sense to me, because there are much scarier things than trust. I wanted to ask him about that, but Mom said we had to go, and now the question has been ringing in my head all night.

I just can't stop thinking: How could trust possibly hurt you?

Now

5

While Mom and a group of parents search for Jennifer, Dad drives me home. He tries to talk, but I tell him I'm exhausted and disappear into my bedroom as soon as we get back.

Right away, I text the group chat: Where do you think she went?

Usually Tess responds first, like, instantly. She's always on her phone, and she types inhumanly fast because she likes to have the first word. But today my question stares back at me, lonely on the screen. A minute goes by, then two.

I switch over to my private text with Reagan and type, You okay?—but that seems wrong. Trying again, I tap out, What are you thinking? I send the message before I can second-guess it, and then I immediately regret it.

Three dots tell me Reagan is typing. Then she deletes it. I stare down at my phone, as if I can scare a response out of it. But my hands are shaking too much to be intimidating.

I sit down on my bed and force deep breaths.

I don't normally feel so out of place with my friends, but everything is different tonight. Against my better judgment, I send Reagan another text. Well . . . that was wild.

Reagan responds right away: Wild?

I realize my mistake. That's Jennifer's word.

Weird, I correct.

No dots this time.

I stare at my silent phone, and when she doesn't text back for six long minutes, I send, How do you feel?

It would be a cringey thing to ask even if Reagan weren't semi-ignoring me, but the question keeps bouncing around in my head.

If this night had gone the way it was supposed to, Reagan and I would be curled up under my covers, trading secrets and stories. And I'd feel the way I always feel during those Reagan late-nights, like we exist in an invisible bubble where we don't have to worry about my mom, or Reagan's dad, or the kids at school who don't really get us. In that bubble, everything is okay because it's just *us*.

But all I have now is silence. The stress of waiting—for a response, for news, for something—is so intense that it twists around my stomach and pulls. To distract myself, I Google stories of girls running away, but that makes me feel much worse.

Time slips as I scroll, and when I hear a knock on my door, I'm so twisted-tense that I actually scream.

The door opens and Dad stands there, brows pinched. "Mal, you should eat something." He walks to the bed, holding out a plate of pork and sauerkraut.

If Mom's pies are a bad sign, Dad's sauerkraut is a bad-news billboard. He says it reminds him of his parents, and he only makes it on the worst days, when we need extra comfort.

I take the plate, and after a bite, warmth spreads through me. "Have you heard from Mom?"

He hesitates before nodding. "They haven't found Jennifer yet."

I already knew that, but after hearing him confirm it, I don't think I can eat any more. I push my sauerkraut away. "Where are they searching? Maybe they're not looking in the right place."

Dad considers this. "Rebecca Chan is with them. The police are investigating. Everyone's sharing any information they have, and everyone's doing what they can."

I stare out my window, into the darkness, and a new, unknowable feeling builds in my chest. "She's just out there, by herself?"

Dad follows my gaze and we sit in silence, as if we're waiting for something to happen, as if Jennifer might pop up and shout, *Gotcha!*

"It's scary," Dad says, in his careful way.

Back when Mom and I were closer, Dad and I didn't talk much. He kept to the sidelines, chiming in with little comments as Mom spoke. But as Mom and I grew apart, Dad filled the space. I've gotten used to his long pauses by now.

Finally, he continues. "But from what I know, Jennifer ran away before, and she came home after a few days."

"But why? Why would she run?"

Dad shakes his head. "That's not my question to answer."

"You mean it's a question for God?"

Dad's lips lift just the slightest bit. Dad believes in God. Mom doesn't. And though they've always left my belief up to me, I don't get how either of them can be so certain. I just believe in *I don't know.*

"That's not what I meant, actually," Dad says.

I wait for him to elaborate, but he doesn't. Sometimes Dad does this kinda annoying thing where he lets a question hang and waits for other people to draw their own conclusions.

But *I don't know.* I don't know what I'm supposed to ask to find the right answer. "Do you mean it's a question for Jennifer?"

He kisses the top of my head, and though I think that's a yes, a thought nags at me.

The way he said it, I thought for a moment he meant it was a question for me. But that wouldn't make sense, because I don't know why she ran. I don't have any idea.

But also, a small part of me whispers, *maybe, just maybe, I might have a guess.*

Because there might be two possible reasons.

One of those is aliens.

And the other is me.

Then

6

Jennifer and I saw each other almost every day the week she moved in. Mostly she came over when she was bored of unpacking—and by *came over,* I mean she walked right into my house and talked with Mom while they waited for me to leave my room.

And because Mom didn't respond to my suggestions of locking the door or telling Jennifer to go home, I didn't have much of a choice.

But the main problem wasn't Jennifer's lack of boundaries. The main problem was that she talked about mind-bending things, like dark energy and altruistic aliens. Even though I obviously didn't believe the alien stuff, the things she said made me feel both scared and excited in a way I couldn't really explain. I just knew I wanted to hear more.

"I think it's time for a sleepover," she declared after a week of coming over unannounced. "It's time to show you some aliens."

And what could I say to that?

A thing about me that I don't really like: I'm not great at sleeping over.

Reagan and I had sleepovers constantly, but she always slept at my house, because even though her house was really nice, her dad always came home late, or sometimes not at all, and Reagan preferred to get away.

I certainly didn't mind. I know I'm way too old to be nervous about sleeping over at someone's house, but it's just . . . more comfortable to be in my own space, where I know where everything is and I can ask my parents for something if I need it.

I wasn't about to tell Jennifer all that, though, because it's embarrassing, and anyway, my house was *right across the street*. So that's how I ended up in a tent, in her backyard, at 10 p.m. on the last Friday of summer.

She'd filled the tent with bottled lemonade, bags of cheese puffs, and boxes of Pocky. She'd also lined the edges with a strand of twinkling fairy lights because, as she said, *If you could surround yourself with stars, why wouldn't you?*

Despite my sleepover anxiety, I felt almost comfortable. And thankfully, the Florida humidity had given us a break tonight, too, because apparently not even the weather could say no to Jennifer Chan.

She turned to me as we lay in our sleeping bags, staring up at the sky through the clear plastic tarp. Half of her hair had escaped its ponytail—and she wore a neon-orange T-shirt that read: ALIENS WALK AMONG US!

"It's wild, isn't it?" she asked. "How bright the stars are?"

To be honest, the lights in Jennifer's house were still on, so the stars didn't look *that* bright, but that seemed like a pretty awful thing to say, so I nodded.

"And is that a shooting star?"

"Um, yeah, maybe," I said, though I hadn't seen anything.

"Maybe it's the start of a meteor shower," Jennifer said, her voice tumbling into excitement. "I've never seen one, but I heard you get them here sometimes. I've always thought that would be the best time to contact aliens, when the sky has opened up."

"Yeah . . . we get them sometimes." Thinking about meteor showers made me think of Reagan—of the sky lighting up outside while we lay in my bed together. It was the first time I saw her scared.

"You're the only person I trust," Reagan had said. "You just get me."

I'd never had a *person* like that before, and it was a relief. "Same for me," I'd responded.

And she'd grinned. "It's us against the world. No one else."

Now, under the light of the not-so-bright stars, Jennifer turned to me. "I'm so glad I met you. I was worried I wouldn't make friends when I moved here."

I tried to smile, but it felt more like a grimace. "I'm sure you'll make other friends at school."

Jennifer beamed. "And I'm so lucky I found a friend who believes in *aliens*."

I swallowed, realizing that I maybe . . . wasn't the person she thought I was. I kept hanging out with Jennifer because something about her was interesting and different. But I wasn't like her.

"You can make other friends, too, though," I said. "Friends that might not need to know about the alien thing. Like, you don't have to tell people or, you know, wear that shirt. That can stay between us."

She paused. "But what if other people want to help us with our search?"

"It's just . . . some people might think the alien stuff is weird."

"But it's not weird."

"*I* know that. But don't you care what people think?"

A shadow passed over her face, but she shook it off. "Some people care about that, but I don't. It doesn't have anything to do with who I am."

"Doesn't it?" I had to make her understand that this mattered—what people thought had *everything* to do with who she was. Because how do we know who we are without knowing our place in the world?

She didn't answer. Instead, she kicked her feet up in the air, pressing her toes against the plastic. "My great-aunt left us this house when she died, and my mom was already struggling to afford Chicago, so we moved here. I'd only visited my great-aunt once, years ago, but I just got this vibe at first, like this whole town was different from me."

My heart pounded. Should I tell her we *were* different from her? I was worried that she wouldn't fit in—at least not if she acted so . . . like herself. Would it be mean to tell her?

Or was that actually the kindest thing to do—to help her, to prepare her?

"So, yeah, I was a little worried. But that's not what's really important," she continued. "Because I also know this place is special. I know it's where I'm meant to be."

I hesitated before asking, "Why?"

"Because there are aliens here. That one time I visited, we were driving nearby, a little past the military base, when suddenly the radio went staticky. And that's when I saw *evidence.*"

I blinked. It was like Jennifer and I existed in two different realities, and I just wanted to drag her back to mine. "Evidence . . . ," I repeated finally.

She leaned forward and said, in an exaggerated whisper, *"Crop circles."*

I frowned. I'd never heard of crop circles in Nowhereville. This was an in-between town. Halfway between Orlando and Tampa, we were surrounded by theme parks and beaches and all the bizarre Florida stories the internet liked to meme—but we claimed none of them as our own. Here was a whole lot of nothing. "Are you sure—?"

But then the lights in Jennifer's house flicked off, and she sat up, grinning in the moonlight. *"Now* we can look."

She closed her eyes and put her hands in the air with her palms facing up. Then she started exhaling in short, fast breaths. *Whoosh, whoosh, whoosh.*

I stared at her. "What are you doing?"

She smiled. "I'm opening myself up to the possibilities."

Who *was* this person, and how had she landed in Nowhereville? I couldn't imagine myself ever doing something like that, even if nobody could see me.

I felt a cloud of secondhand embarrassment, followed by worry and the need to protect her. But then came a sharper feeling, too, like a shard of glass in a box of cotton balls.

Annoyance, almost. Because *she* should have felt embarrassed and worried. She should've been protecting herself. It didn't seem fair for her to ignore all the things that mattered.

For whatever reason, the universe decided that I had to worry, all the time, about how things looked and what people thought, and Jennifer just . . . didn't.

It almost felt like she was rubbing that in my face.

When she finished *whoosh-whoosh*ing, she scrambled out of the tent, and I followed her onto the lawn, still damp from the afternoon rain.

"What possibilities, exactly?" I felt like I was always ten steps behind her, sprinting to catch up.

"A *sighting*." Jennifer tipped her head to the sky. "You look for a bright ball of light, usually red or white, flashing three times and moving in a way you can't explain. Sometimes you'll be able to see the actual aircraft, possibly shaped like an oval or a Tic Tac. But most important, you look for . . . a feeling. You'll know it when you feel it. You'll be sure, sure up to Jupiter and back."

Something about that phrase settled inside me. It just felt so *Jennifer*. Reagan has a whole thing about words and phrases. She said most people follow trends, but the best people set them. And Reagan was always setting trends with

40

words. *It's the coolest thing,* she once said, *to worm your way into how people think.*

"But how do you really *know* something?" I asked Jennifer.

She smiled at my uncertainty, like it was cute. And *that—* that was what I meant by *rubbing it in.* "Have you read the journal I gave you?" she asked.

"Uh . . ." I'd read the first couple entries. But then I just . . . couldn't. Reading it felt like intruding. Her writing was so personal, and I could feel her *wanting* in every single word. It almost hurt to read.

"Don't you think there could be an earthly explanation for all this?" I asked.

"There are over one hundred billion galaxies in the universe. And each of those galaxies contains one hundred billion stars."

I looked up at the sky, trying to comprehend just how big the universe actually was. It made my brain numb.

"So there must be another civilization out there," she continued. "There must be *multiple* civilizations. In that infinite universe, is it really so hard to believe there'd be one species who wants to reach out? Who wants to show us that we aren't alone?"

As I stared up at the stars, they seemed to get just a tiny bit brighter. "I guess not," I admitted.

"I'm not the only one."

I looked back at her, and for the first time, she looked truly frustrated. "It's real, Mallory. We know it's real. So many people have *seen* unidentified aerial phenomena. The government even confirmed the existence of UAPs! And yet people refuse to care."

"Couldn't there be a whole lot of explanations? We don't know for sure that it's—"

"There's a whole team of scientists listening to the sky, trying to hear aliens. Scientists have transmitters that point into space to record anything unusual. And you know what? They *found* something."

I hesitated. "They found something in . . . space?"

She nodded. "Back in the seventies, scientists set up a radio telescope called the Big Ear. For months, the Ear listened without finding anything. But one night, it picked up a signal, coming from the stars. The signal lasted for seventy-two seconds, and it was thirty times louder and clearer than anything they'd ever heard before."

"And what was it?"

"That's the thing. The scientist on duty that night was so shocked that he printed out the recording and wrote 'Wow!' next to it. To this day, he and his team still think aliens are the best possible explanation."

I looked back at the sky, and fear tickled my heart. "So what did they do?"

"Nothing."

"What?" I turned back to her. "But if they thought it was aliens, shouldn't they have . . . looked into it?"

She sighed. "They didn't have enough money. Programs like that don't get a lot of funding, not when the country has to pay for the military and stuff. Humans would rather spend their money creating bombs and death than searching for *life*."

I opened and closed my mouth. "But . . . we need to know about this stuff."

Her lips lifted again. She could never hold her smile back for long. "*See?* This is what I mean. This is why it's up to us."

That didn't seem right to me. It shouldn't be up to us. We were just kids.

But before I could say that, Jennifer opened her arms wide and shouted to the stars, "Hello, aliens! We are here! We believe in you!" Her words were so loud that they echoed through the empty neighborhood.

I clapped my hand over my mouth, as if *I* were the one shouting into the night. "What are you *doing*?" I whispered. We'd been talking at a normal volume, but after that I felt like I had to make myself barely audible, just to balance her out.

"Sometimes you have to announce yourself, you know?"

I did not know.

"You just have to put it into the universe." She grinned at my disbelief, trying not to laugh. "It's fun. Try it."

I glanced up at her mom's dark window and around our silent neighborhood. Everything was the way it always was. Sleepy houses dozed on manicured lawns. Matching mailboxes guarded homes like watchdogs. Faded American flags drooped in the breezeless night.

Even though no one was around, I suddenly got this fear that someone at school might find out. It was the feeling I got sometimes, as if everyone was watching me. As if I had an invisible audience that I had to be aware of, always.

Jennifer nudged me. "You don't have to be so afraid, you know."

Reagan taught me tricks, ways to live in the world so I wouldn't have to worry, ways to make sure other people thought good things about me, so I didn't have to stress about their opinions.

But Jennifer made me feel, almost, like there was nothing to worry about in the first place. Like I didn't have to learn any special tricks; I just had to *be*. Like everything important in the universe was right there in front of me, waiting for me to see it.

"Say something," she whispered.

I took a deep breath. I opened my arms wide. The words built up in my chest. *I'm here. I believe.*

I really thought I might say the words.

But I couldn't. "No thanks," I said, dropping my arms. "That's not really me."

Jennifer tilted her head. "It could be."

When I didn't respond, her brows pinched, and I turned back to the sky to avoid her pity.

As I looked up at the stars, I felt myself holding my breath, straining to see something different, searching my heart for some kind of *feeling*.

Standing there with her, I could almost forget everything I knew about how the world worked. And that's what was so scary about being her friend.

Jennifer made me want to believe.

Now

7

I can't sleep.

When Mom comes home, Dad tells her I'm in bed, and she leaves me be. The hours tick away. I chase sleep but can't catch it.

Every time I close my eyes, I think of the Incident. Every time the house creaks or the wind whistles outside, I hear *Jennifer Chan is missing.*

For hours, I scroll on my phone, trying to ignore the tight fist of worry smashing my internal organs—and I'm so busy distracting myself that I almost don't notice.

I almost don't see the light outside—not until a beam of red swings into my room, illuminating my white walls, desk, and bed in an eerie glow. It's like, suddenly, I'm inside a haunted house.

I grasp for my blanket and pull it over my head, embarrassed by my reaction. It's just *light*. Probably light from the search party. That would make sense.

But I can't escape the fear that seizes me. The light seeps

through the cotton of my comforter. Then it flashes. Once. Twice. Three times.

And it disappears.

With deep breaths, I sit up and push the covers off me. If I was awake before, I'm wired now. Already, I'm working out how to tell this story to my friends. I'm wondering if they'd care, or if they'd think I was reacting to nothing.

But that was something.

Almost against my will, I slide out of bed and nudge my window open with slippery, sweating hands.

Outside, the world is empty and silent, and I begin to wonder if I imagined the flashing light entirely.

"Hello?" I whisper.

Nothing.

I crane my neck toward the sky, feeling silly—and then annoyed. Angry. Because what if that *was* something? What if somehow, impossibly, Jennifer was right?

What if extraterrestrial beings showed up at my window, and all I did was hide under the covers?

Before I can stop myself, I hoist my legs over the window-sill and jump out, landing barefoot on the crunchy brown grass beneath my room.

It's not a far jump. My room is on the first floor, and it's only elevated by a few steps. But still, I've never climbed out a window before. I've certainly never snuck out of one.

I take a few steps away from my house, into my back-yard. Nothing's there, and I don't know if I feel relief or disappointment.

I turn to go back inside—

And then the air seems to thicken into paste. It grows clingy, sticking to my skin, and a bead of sweat tickles as it slides down my back. This humidity is so heavy that I find it hard to breathe.

I should be used to this heat. It gets this bad during the summer, on the worst days. But it's already October, and this feels different. This feels . . . wild.

Adrenaline speeds through my veins, urging me to dive right through my window and back under my covers. But I fight it, forcing myself to look up.

In the inky sky, a red oval of light, big as a helicopter but long and slim as a Tic Tac, blips into existence, blocking out the thin sliver of moon. It hovers above the oak trees, too far to reach, but still much too close for comfort. I glance around for anybody else, but there's no one.

Then the Tic Tac dips and swerves, flitting through the neighborhood. I watch as it skims over the shingled roofs, moving faster than anything I've ever seen, zipping up and down as if gravity does not apply.

When it stops, it floats right above me. The light illuminates my body, and I freeze, staring at my hands. They look like they've been dipped in blood.

Fear fizzes like ginger ale in my stomach—so bubbly I could almost mistake it for excitement.

"Jennifer?" Her name escapes my lips as I stare up, wondering what this thing is, where it came from—and what, or who, is inside it.

I raise a hand to shield my eyes from the light, and one side of the Tic Tac lifts, mirroring me. Slowly, I lower that hand and raise the other, and the Tic Tac tilts the other way, mirroring me again.

My breath quickens. My heart thuds. "What do you want?" I whisper.

The light flashes again. Once. Twice. Three times. And then the UAP is gone, leaving me standing alone, sweat dampened and suddenly far too cold.

I wrap my arms around myself to keep from shivering, gulping air as my eyes adjust to the dark.

There must be an explanation. An *earthly* explanation. Because even if aliens *did* exist, they wouldn't come to Nowhereville. They wouldn't come to *me*. It's not possible.

But as I stare up at the now-empty sky, a tiny part of me whispers, *The world isn't what you thought it was.*

Something infinite and burning expands inside me. A big bang, of sorts.

"That really happened," I whisper to the silent night. "And I know why Jennifer left."

But who could I possibly tell? Nobody would ever believe I saw aliens.

Jennifer Chan's Guide to the Universe
Volume VII, Entry No. 1: How to Tell If You've Been Contacted by Aliens

1. Animals notice first. If birds stop chirping and dogs stop barking, be alert! Aliens are here.
2. Unidentified Friendly Objects will naturally affect Earth's atmosphere, so pay attention to the air around you! Do you notice an increase or decrease in temperature? Can you catch the scent of rain? Is your nose starting to tingle, like you're about to sneeze or maybe even cry?
3. If you're near a radio, you will hear static, three beeps, and maybe even a secret message! This will probably give you a headache.
4. You will see a blinking light in the sky. Once. Twice. Then a third time. This is their signal. It means they're ready.

Important Note: Many people are afraid of aliens, but there is no need for this! It's like Dad told me when we went stargazing. Caution is advised, of course, but think about this: aliens have planned their contact for longer than you've even been <u>alive,</u> and they only have one chance to get it right. Which means they chose <u>you.</u> If they pick

you, then they must have a good reason. You must be
special.

   And think about this, too: if aliens chose you, if they
trusted you, that's a big responsibility. So ask yourself one
very important question: How are you going to live up to it?

Now

8

The whole school is full of buzz.

Fifteen minutes before the first bell, everyone's talking about Jennifer—about why she ran and where she went.

She's a celebrity now, apparently, but I'm not interested in rumors.

I hurry past the picnic tables at the front of the school, where kids are gathering to share whispers and theories, and I burst into the main building. My friends are leaning against the lockers.

"Mal, thank god you're here." Reagan grins when she sees me, genuine relief in her voice, and I smile for the first time since we heard the news. Despite everything, I feel myself relaxing.

"Tess is being a nightmare," Reagan says.

"Rude," Tess responds, though she doesn't seem all that bothered.

"Kidding." Reagan flashes Tess a grin before slipping into a frown. "But I was so worried about Jennifer last night. I could barely sleep. And now Tess won't stop talking about her."

Hearing this, I'm so relieved I could cry. I'm not the only one who's worried. "Same," I say. "Actually, in the middle of the night, I—"

Tess interrupts. "Have you heard the latest? Erika Rose saw Jennifer by the Wells Fargo after school yesterday, so we think she might have robbed a bank and that's why she ran?"

Reagan gives the world's longest sigh. "See what I've been dealing with, Mal? Tess, that's ridiculous. You know that's ridiculous."

Tess's eyes widen. "How should *I* know what's true or not? I just wouldn't put it past her, is all."

"Please," Reagan scoffs. "How would she rob a bank? She's *twelve*."

"I'm just saying. My mom's been concerned about Jennifer from the beginning. She says the parenting is questionable, and we don't trust anyone who doesn't go to church."

Reagan and I exchange a glance, and Tess raises her hands. "Except you two, of course!"

Reagan rolls her eyes. "Tess, the girl ran away. Don't over-complicate this."

I bite my lip. "But do you think maybe . . ."

Tess tilts her head, expectant. Reagan's eyes narrow.

I hesitate. "Maybe this has to do with aliens?"

I'm met with blank stares.

"Do you think . . . ," I add quietly, even though everything in me is screaming *STOP TALKING*, "that aliens found her?"

Reagan turns to Tess, whose mouth has fallen open in disgust, and says, "Excuse us."

Then she grabs my wrist and leads me through the crowd of students, out of the main building, and toward the chapel. We patter down the steps to the basement and stumble into the girls' bathroom. Nobody ever uses it, so it's where we go when things are serious. Where nobody can overhear us.

This bathroom keeps secrets.

After the door swings shut and Reagan makes sure the stalls are empty, I blurt, "I saw something last night. And I know I sound like a walnu—weird, but I think it might lead us to Jennifer. I think we can—"

"Mal." Reagan cuts me off, brows pinched. "I'm worried."

"Me too! Tess doesn't get it, but I think there's a way we can help Jennifer."

"No." Reagan reaches for me. "I'm worried about *you*. Mal, I love you, but you need to get a grip."

Without thinking, I take a step back, bumping into the wall behind me. For a moment my mind flashes to Jennifer, pressed up against the bathroom sinks, staring at us. I slide to the tiled floor, ignoring the germs.

Reagan sits next to me. "Look, Mal, of course I'm worried about Jennifer. She's out there alone, and she seems a little, you know . . . unstable. But your brand of worry is different. It always has been." Her eyes soften. "Remember how bad it was before we became friends? You overthought everything."

I nod, remembering Reagan during those sleepovers, just weeks after we met. It was like someone finally saw me, offered to carry a load of my anxieties and threw away the rest.

You don't have to worry anymore, she said. *I've got your back.*

And in return, I had hers.

Reagan scoots closer to me. "Think about this logically. This isn't the first time Jennifer's run away, and it won't be the last. This has nothing to do with you."

I let her words wash over me. Maybe they're true. Maybe it's just a coincidence that she ran right after the Incident.

I close my eyes and push Jennifer into a tiny corner of my brain. I shove the door closed on the thoughts of what we did, like a closet overflowing with dirty clothes. Space opens up in my heart, and when I don't have to worry about Jennifer, I can breathe again.

But that door won't stay shut. Sighing, I open my eyes. "It's just that she ran away a few days after we—"

"Talked to her?" Reagan finishes. "Mal, that's all we did. We talked. And if she's fragile enough to let that bother her, she has bigger problems than just us."

I stare at a crack on the floor, tracing the jagged path with my eyes, all the way to the wall. What Reagan's saying might be true. But I ask, "Shouldn't we try to find her?"

Reagan sighs. "Mal, what will people think if you're running around talking about her? You'll look guilty—and I know you always second-guess everything, but I'm telling you: you don't have to. You're the nicest person I know."

"But—"

"And you don't want to make this a *thing.*"

"Right." My voice sounds almost robotic.

Reagan stands, holding out a hand, and I take it. But even as I try to convince Reagan that I'll let this go, I can't stop thinking about what I saw last night.

I can't stop thinking about Jennifer.

All the way down in my gut, I know: I need to tell someone what happened.

If my friends won't listen, I need to find people who will. And as much as I hate it, I know that's Ingrid Stone and Kath Abrams.

The problem is, going to Ingrid would be betraying Reagan. It would mean taking a step backward, toward the person I used to be—toward a person I never wanted to be again.

Then

9

When I met Reagan, I was about to faint for the second time in my life.

The first time was in fifth grade, when Mom, Dad, and I had driven to the Florida State Fair. It had cotton candy, and neon lights, and cartoon drawings of Florida that looked alarmingly like guns—but most important was the Ferris wheel. I was thrilled to ride it, until we got to the top.

"Look at all the lights," Mom said, pointing to the fair beneath us. I peeked out of our cart, and there below us was the biggest carnival I'd ever been to.

Except, from that high, it didn't look big at all. Actually, it looked kind of small. And I had the weirdest feeling that I still can't really explain. Like I was some monster giant, and the whole world had shrunk beneath me. Like, one wrong step and I'd crush everything.

My breath quickened, and my palms got sweaty, and I was honestly pretty used to those things, because I got scared kind of a lot. But this time was worse. This time I was looking at the world and realizing it was so much different than I'd thought. I couldn't breathe.

Then the next thing I knew, I was lying on the floor of our carriage, and we'd circled to the bottom of the ride again. The whole wheel had stopped, and some stranger was peering over me, saying, "She's okay. She just fainted. I think she was afraid."

I wanted to explain that I wasn't just *afraid*. It was bigger than that. It was as if I'd discovered something terrible, some horrible secret about the universe and myself.

But once I was off that ride, back on solid ground, I couldn't exactly remember that discovery, and I didn't want to think about it. I just vowed to never go that high again.

And that was never a problem until the first day of sixth grade, when we were in PE and our task was to climb to the top of a rope.

I was eight people away from having to climb, and every time the line moved up, I felt a fresh wave of nausea. My armpits prickled. My heart raced. I knew if I climbed that rope, I might faint at the top, which meant I would *fall and die*. So the stakes were high. Literally.

I considered telling someone, but my fear felt too embarrassing to admit, and I wasn't close enough with anyone in my PE class. I wasn't very close with anyone in general. I was really only friends with Ingrid, who was too fearless to confess these things to. And Tess, who was kind of friends with everybody but who also didn't seem to like me.

When I was fourth in line, someone tapped me on the

shoulder, and I turned to see Reagan, the new girl. I'd been so freaked about the rope that I hadn't even noticed her behind me. If I hadn't been so panicked, I would've been excited because so far, the rumors were fascinating. She was from Philadelphia, which was cool enough on its own. But also, Tess told me, her mom had been struck by lightning, which was unique in a morbid kind of way.

"Are you okay?" Reagan asked.

I nodded, because the only thing worse than being scared was admitting you were scared.

"Are you sure? Because you look like you might drop dead."

I gulped, like, audibly.

Reagan raised her eyebrows. "Should I tell a teacher?"

I shook my head. "No, no. I'm just . . . nervous." I admitted it not because I wanted to, but because I couldn't think of anything else to say.

Her eyes narrowed. "About heights?"

"It's not a big deal," I lied. We moved up another space in line.

"Climbing a *rope* isn't a big deal. But being afraid is. You shouldn't have to do this if you're scared."

It hadn't occurred to me that I had a choice.

"Follow me." Her lips lifted into the slightest smile. "I have a plan."

"Wait," I said, worried that she might tell the class how scared I was. But when she walked out of line and up to our PE teacher, I followed.

"Ms. Crabb," Reagan said, putting on a pained smile and dropping her voice to a whisper. "This is kind of embarrassing, but we just got our periods."

I felt my cheeks go hot, because getting your period in gym class was way more humiliating than being scared of heights, and I was afraid Ms. Crabb might announce *that* to the class. Also . . . it was a lie, and I wasn't very good at lying.

Our teacher pursed her lips, as if she'd heard this trick a million times. "*Both* of you?"

Reagan nodded solemnly. "It happens when girls spend a lot of time together."

"Reagan Sullivan, right? Aren't you new?" The line of Ms. Crabb's lips got thinner, and I thought she was angry until I realized she was trying not to laugh.

Reagan sighed. "Yes, and this is a pretty rough way to start my time here, to be honest. Can we go to the health center to lie down? The cramps are very painful."

Ms. Crabb turned to me, and I smiled. Then frowned. I wasn't sure how a girl who just got her period might look.

She stared at us for a long time, and my heart beat wildly. What would the punishment be if she found out we were lying? Either way, I was in this with Reagan now—and I really didn't want to climb that rope.

Finally, Ms. Crabb nodded. "You may go straight to the health center and lie down for the rest of gym hour. If you really do have your period, ask Nurse Lila for Advil and a pad."

Nurse Lila clearly didn't believe us. She had a reputation for sensing when kids were lying about pains and illnesses. But since we'd already gotten permission from Ms. Crabb, she just gestured to the cots.

"I can't believe that happened," Reagan whisper-laughed as we lay in the back of the health center. "I saw that on TV before, but I didn't think it would work in real life."

"I thought you must have done that so many times," I marveled. "You seemed so confident."

"So did you," she said. That probably wasn't true, but when she said it, I almost believed it.

"I've never even gotten my period," I confessed, cheeks heating. That wasn't the kind of thing you were supposed to *tell* people—especially not people you just met. But there was something about Reagan that felt like cinnamon-apple pie. She made me feel safe.

"Me neither." She scooted closer to me. "Don't tell anyone."

"Of course not."

She grinned, and friendship suddenly felt easy. This was what people looked for—someone who chose you and got you and made all your worries seem smaller.

"Look at us," she said. "Partners in crime."

Reagan and I hung out every day after that, and she started sleeping over a lot, but it wasn't until three months later that we solidified our forever friendship.

We were lying in my bed late at night, talking about which

guys she had a crush on (she was still deciding between Kyle and Pete), when suddenly she went silent.

"What's wrong?" I asked.

She stared out my window like she'd seen, well, an alien. "Do you see that? In the distance?"

I squinted and saw streaks of light, zipping through the darkness. "Shooting stars!"

"Right."

It took me a minute to realize that for Reagan, shooting stars were *not* a good thing. It seemed pretty weird to have a grudge against shooting stars, but it probably wasn't any weirder than having a grudge against Ferris wheels.

"What's wrong?" I asked.

She turned to me, her back to the window. "Can you keep a secret?"

I nodded. I'd been keeping her secrets for months now. Nobody else knew about her crushes.

"My mom didn't get hit by lightning."

"Oh." Now that she said it, I felt kinda guilty for believing it. "Yeah, I figured it was just a rumor someone started."

"I started it."

"Oh."

"I mentioned it to Tess Vance in first period, and by the afternoon, everyone knew. We should hang out with her more. She's the kind of person who's great as a friend and terrible as an enemy."

I laughed, then hesitated. "But . . . why'd you start it?"

She shrugged. "I gave people something to talk about. Better than letting someone *else* make up stories."

"Right." I guess when she put it that way, it made sense.

"My mom left us," she said finally.

My breath caught in my throat. I'd been fighting a lot with Mom recently, but I couldn't imagine her *leaving*. "I'm so sorry."

"She left during a meteor shower, which was a bummer. I ran to her room to tell her about it, and I was so excited—kind of pathetic in hindsight, like, it's just space junk—but she was gone."

"That's terrible," I whispered.

Reagan shifted the blanket between us. "I was super young, honestly, so it doesn't matter." Except it did matter. I could tell. And it wasn't just the fact that she'd told me—it was also the fact that *I could tell*. I could read her, and she *let* me read her. That felt like a gift. And I felt special.

"Nobody stays forever," she said. "You can't trust anyone."

"You can trust me."

I didn't know how to show her just how much I meant that, but I think she understood. It wasn't her popularity that made me want to be her friend. It wasn't her get-out-of-PE schemes or her confidence or her wisdom. It was that everyone else—my parents and Ingrid and the other kids at school—looked at me and saw a scared little girl who fainted on Ferris wheels and turned bright red when the teacher called on her. But when Reagan looked at me, she saw someone different. Someone brave and fun and trustworthy.

As stardust sprinted through the sky outside, I promised her, "I'll stay."

Now
10

I know who I need to ask for help. I just don't want to.

After school ends, I'm taking some deep breaths in front of room 204—the official home of the Science Club. I asked Mom and Dad to pick me up a little late today because I had a project to do—which is *kind of* true.

All I have to do now is open the door and say *Hi, Ingrid. Hi, Kath. Something happened last night.*

If anyone can help me find Jennifer, it's these two. Ingrid's got this laser-beam kind of smart, especially when it comes to science. She focuses on one thing at a time and researches and experiments until she knows everything about it.

Kath's brand of smart is more zoomed out. She's the first-chair violinist and president of the Audio Tech Club. She's also the type of kid who can take an assignment, look at it from a ton of different angles, and come up with an approach nobody else even thought of. Our teachers praise her for being *outside the box,* which makes me a little uncomfortable, because she's Black and Jewish in a mostly white, Christian school, and sometimes I wonder if they just mean *different*.

I check the time on my phone. I've been standing in front of this door for four whole minutes. Anybody watching would be completely weirded out. But luckily, room 204 is tucked away in a forgotten hallway on the second floor.

I'm about to go inside—I really am—when the door swings open to reveal Kath standing in front of me, looking just as startled as I feel.

"Um." Her black Afro spills out from under the hood of her army jacket, which she tugs further up over her head. "Hi?"

"Hi." I force a smile. The muscles in my cheeks twitch.

She stares at me, and there's an uncomfortable silence until I realize I'm supposed to keep talking. "I just wanted to talk to Ingrid?" I say, only it sounds like I'm asking for permission.

I've never had a conversation with Kath outside of class, and there's that underlying awkwardness of being in totally different friend groups.

"Okay, well, she's busy with Science Club right now. And you're not part of Science Club. So . . . bye," she says before closing the door in my face.

I stand there, stunned. That was so . . . *weird*? Plus, the "Science Club" only consists of Ingrid and Kath. Everybody knows it's just a way for them to get club credit while they hang out and Ingrid messes with lab equipment.

I chew my lip.

If Reagan were here, she wouldn't listen to Kath. Whatever

Reagan wanted, she would make happen, and she wouldn't let anyone stand in her way.

So I'm about to barge in—*really,* I am—when the door opens again, and Kath frowns.

"I'm not letting you in," she explains. "I'm just going to the bathroom. That's why I opened the door in the first place, but you distracted me. Anyway, you still can't go inside."

She steps around me and walks down the hallway, glancing over her shoulder to make sure I don't enter the classroom.

I wait until she turns the corner and consider giving up, before I realize I'm being ridiculous. Kath can't lock me out of a *classroom.*

When I step inside, I see Ingrid bent over a microscope, facing away from me. Ms. Rodgers is sitting in the back of the room, but she's super old and nearly deaf, so I don't worry about her. I don't even think she knows I entered, because she doesn't look up from her book.

I clear my throat. "Hey . . . there."

When Ingrid doesn't turn around, I realize she's wearing earplugs. I forgot about that. Ingrid can only think in complete silence.

I walk across the room, hoping she'll just *sense* my presence, but she still doesn't turn. Not sure what else to do, I tap her on the shoulder.

She screams and whips around, and I stumble backward, banging my hip against one of the desks.

Instinctively, we both turn to Ms. Rodgers, but she just licks a finger and flips a page like nothing happened.

"I'm sorry!" I throw my hands up as if to say, *I come in peace.* "Don't freak out. I just wanted—"

Ingrid tugs out her earplugs. "You almost gave me a freaking heart attack. I'm a little on edge after . . ." She pauses, a Jennifer-sized hole in the conversation. And then: "What are you doing here? I mean . . . what are *you* doing *here*?"

I clear my throat. "Something happened last night."

She squints and leans back, resting a hand on the table behind her. "Okaaay."

The spark of interest on her face is so familiar that for a second, she's the old Ingrid again. It's almost as if the last year never happened, as if she still likes me.

"It'saboutJennifer." I'm talking super fast. My words are blurring together. "And I know you were friends with her, so I thought you might—"

Ingrid interrupts, confused. "I wasn't friends with Jennifer."

I pause. "But she sat with you and Kath at lunch. I thought you guys . . ." Who did Jennifer hang out with, if not Kath and Ingrid? Did she have any friends at all?

Ingrid shakes her head. "She ate lunch with us that first week, but I guess she wasn't interested in being friends, because she just stopped. I liked her, though."

I was so sure Jennifer was hanging out with Kath and Ingrid. Jennifer had friends—I'd made sure of that.

"Well, regardless," I say after a moment's silence, "if anyone can figure this out, it's you."

The crease between Ingrid's brows deepens. "Why do you think that?"

"Because I've seen you when you're trying to find an-swers."

When we were younger, Ingrid was always getting in trouble for conducting over-the-top science experiments, just because she was curious about the world. One time, she even set a controlled fire at Howard Park because she wanted to test how to handle forest fires. She burned our initials into the field—for science—but when she put it out, the burnt re-mains just looked like wobbly lines. You could only tell they were letters if you squinted.

"I know you," I add. We may not be friends anymore, but we hung out enough—which has to count for something.

Ingrid's shoulders hunch. "You don't, though."

Before I can respond, the door bangs open. Ingrid and I both jump.

"Of course," Kath says, stalking across the room and sinking into one of the desk chairs. "Of course you didn't listen."

Clearly, neither of them wants me here. This was prob-ably a mistake, but I need to try. Jennifer's *missing*. And if I can't ease my way into it, maybe I need to surprise them. Maybe I need to appeal to their *intellectual curiosity*. I blurt, "What if Jennifer found aliens?"

For a while, the only sound in the room is the flick of Ms. Rodgers's book as she obliviously turns the page.

Then Ingrid says, "Aliens?"

And Kath says, "Jennifer?"

The way they're watching me makes me itchy. I can't tell what they're thinking.

I take a breath and force myself to explain. "Jennifer told me what an unidentified aerial phenomenon sighting is like. But I didn't really get it until last night, when I saw this red oval spaceship thing, and everything was weirdly quiet and . . . Anyway, I know it sounds hard to believe, but I'm wondering if aliens really do exist." I glance around, quadruple-checking that none of our classmates are somehow hiding or listening in. "Because if they do, maybe Jennifer didn't run away. Maybe she got abducted."

Kath narrows her eyes. "Is this some horrible joke?"

"No! I'm serious." I hate that Kath thinks I'd joke about this.

Ingrid tilts her head. "Are you sure it wasn't a trick of the light? Some electrical feedback? A helicopter with searchlights? You know the whole town's been looking for her."

When she lays it out like that, in her practical Ingrid way, it seems so obvious. Of course it wasn't aliens.

But still—I can't shake that certainty from last night. I've never seen anything like it. And it's hard to explain that *feeling*, like something completely out of this universe was happening.

It's hard to explain it without sounding like . . . Jennifer.

"I don't think it was a helicopter," I say. "And what if the adults aren't looking in the right place? What if *we* could?"

"So, you want to look . . . in outer space?" Kath doesn't ask it in a mean way. The annoyance on her face has slipped away, and she asks it frankly—a legitimate question.

"Um," I respond, because I don't have a legitimate answer. "Yes?"

Ingrid sighs and I brace myself, waiting for her to kick me out of the classroom.

Then she says, almost reluctantly, "Give me a second," before shoving her earplugs back in. She walks over to the classroom computer and starts typing frantically. Thinking. Searching.

Kath leans forward. She has this burning kind of intensity that's actually not all that different from Reagan's. "So you're for real? You actually believe that aliens are here?"

"I don't know," I admit. "But Jennifer believed it was possible. Nobody believed her before. Nobody took her seriously."

"Including you."

Heat pools behind my cheeks. Sometimes when I don't know how to react, I think about what my friends would do. Tess would clap back. Reagan would make a joke like she didn't care at all.

But neither of those responses seems right.

Instead I say, "Maybe I was wrong."

A flicker of surprise flits across Kath's face, and she's about to say something when Ingrid pulls out her earplugs.

"Okay, look at this," she says, and Kath and I walk over to see that she's got an image of our solar system up on the screen. "It feels like life in space should be more common, but the conditions for supporting life as we know it are really narrow. And really rare."

"But there are a hundred billion galaxies," I say.

Ingrid fiddles with the tiny silver cross on her neck, always a sign that she's trying to figure something out. "True, but in order to support life, a thousand things need to go just right. For instance—" She cuts herself off abruptly and mumbles, "Never mind. You probably don't want to hear all the details."

I'm thrown off by her sudden embarrassment, but Kath nods with understanding. "Yes we do. Go on."

Hesitating a little, Ingrid clears her throat and continues. "Well, okay. Okay. In order to support life, we need a moon, because the moon affects our ocean. But not just any moon, which lots of planets have, but our *exact* moon, at this exact size at this exact distance from Earth. Our moon probably came from another planet colliding with Earth billions of years ago. But it had to hit Earth at a *very* precise angle in order to end up where it did. See?"

She clicks on the image of the moon, and a simulation plays—a collision between Earth and another planet. In the first collision, both planets completely explode. In the next, only a tiny piece of the moon-planet chips off, and the rest keeps hurtling off into space. New simulations play out, each one totally different. None of them create the moon as we know it.

I lean in, like if I get close enough, the screen will tell me what I want to hear. "But other planets must have moons like ours."

"It's not only the moon, though," she says, getting excited again. "It's also the *exact* size and distance of our sun, which puts us in the minuscule sweet spot for liquid water. It's even

Jupiter: having a gas giant at that exact distance essentially serves as a bodyguard, sucking up most of the asteroids that might hit Earth."

"Oh." I feel hope leaking out of me. Maybe this was ridiculous. Believing in aliens was ridiculous.

Seeing my expression, Ingrid's eyes soften. "Look, I'm not saying it's *impossible*. It's just unlikely. When scientists search for extraterrestrial life, they're expecting organisms that are essentially microscopic worms—not spaceship-flying, twelve-year-old-abducting moon-people."

I wince. "Right. Right."

Kath chimes in. "But there must be some scientists who believe in UFO aliens, right?"

I turn to Kath, confused, because it sounds like she's on my side. Kath won't return my glance.

"Well, yes. Lots of things are possible." Ingrid takes a breath. "And we know there *are* unidentified flying objects. The Pentagon confirmed that there are aircraft that fly in ways the government can't explain. They accelerate faster than any technology we currently have, they change directions rapidly, and they seem to disappear."

"Exactly!" I say. "That's aliens."

Ingrid holds up a hand. *Slow down, Mal.* "But unidentified is just that . . . *unidentified*. The UFOs could be technology from other countries. Or technology from our country that the government is lying about. They could even be something from a parallel universe, or a product of time travel."

"This is making aliens sound pretty reasonable," Kath says.

71

"My point is," Ingrid continues, "extraterrestrial life is one explanation for UFOs. But we need to focus on facts, not stories. All the evidence we have points to something unidentified *here*, on Earth. There's no evidence of anything happening out *there*."

"That's not necessarily true." Maybe I'm starting to sound like a conspiracy theorist, but I can't help it. I tell them about the Big Ear and the *Wow!* signal, trying to recall the details.

"It was a seventy-two-second-long beep that nobody could explain, and nobody followed up on it," I finish. "So, I think there's a whole lot going on that we don't know about. Most people don't want to believe in this stuff, but Jennifer's been trying to find the right . . . uh, phone number, or something."

Ingrid and Kath exchange a look—but it's not one that says *She's nuts.*

It's one that says *Could it be?*

"There was a signal that strong? And it wasn't coming from Earth?" Ingrid's fingers find her necklace again. "If that's true . . . and if your UFO sighting is true . . . that does sound like something to look into."

She's intrigued. She's *in.* I'm ready to celebrate until Ingrid pulls back again, embarrassment slamming down over her face. "But I can't."

Involuntarily, I reach forward, as if I could grasp her curiosity and tug it back to the surface. Then I drop my hand. "Why not?"

Her eyes flick away from mine, down to her hands, which she twists in front of her. "I just don't think it's a good idea."

Kath looks at Ingrid. Then looks at me. Her brows knit, and her voice is almost desperate when she says, "I wish we could help."

I'm trying not to panic. I don't know what happened. I was so close to making them understand—so close to getting their help. And I need their help to find Jennifer. I *need* to find Jennifer. "Please," I beg.

Ingrid meets my eyes, and I can't find the girl I was kind of friends with, or even the girl who hates me. This girl just looks empty. "It's not our place to look for Jennifer. Let's just leave this to the professionals and stay out of it."

The Ingrid I knew didn't believe in "staying out" of things. The Ingrid I knew was very *into* things. She was reckless and curious about everything.

And the Ingrid I knew wouldn't stay out of this just because she was mad at me for getting popular. But maybe things have changed more than I realized.

"Think about Jennifer . . . ," I whisper.

Ingrid turns away.

I'm on top of the Ferris wheel again, swaying, looking down at the distant, tiny Earth below. My eyes burn. I take a deep breath to bring me back to now.

"Okay," I say, voice hoarse. And then I leave the room, trying to bury my panic as I walk away. I have to find Jennifer. I have to figure out those lights. But I have no idea how, and no one to turn to.

What would Jennifer do?

The answer to that, of course, is she'd try to find aliens on her own. But I'm not smart enough. I'm not brave enough. I can't—

Behind me, the classroom door slams, and I turn to see Kath, walking toward me with her hands stuffed into her jacket pockets.

"Fine," she says, almost as if it pains her, "I'll help you."

"Really?" Relief nearly knocks me over. For one ridiculous moment, I feel the urge to hug her, but of course I don't. That's not the vibe.

She sighs. "I don't trust you. I don't think you and your friends are nice people."

"Oh." There's not much else to say to that.

"But . . ." She takes a deep breath. "I think you're trying to do the right thing. And when people are trying to do the right thing, it's probably the right thing to help them, right?"

This feels like a trap somehow. I don't want to mess this up. "Right?"

"Don't get too excited, though. I'm great, but I'm not a science expert like Ingrid. I have no clue how to find aliens."

"Me neither." I glance back at the closed classroom door. "Do you think you could convince Ingrid?"

Kath sucks her lips, thinking. "I'll try, but I doubt anything I say will work. She's stubborn when she makes a decision. At this point, it would probably take a miracle for her to say yes."

"All right." I swallow my disappointment, because even if Kath doesn't trust me, even if she doesn't like me, I'm still grateful she's willing to help. "Did Jennifer say *anything* to you that might be helpful? I really thought you hung out with her."

Kath bites her thumbnail. "Not really. I only hung out with her that first week."

I nod. I thought I had everything figured out, but I'm starting to realize, with creeping dread, there's so much I don't know.

Then

11

Jennifer's first day of school started off better than I could have expected. Jennifer's status as new girl made her pseudo-popular, and the rumors only fueled the sense of mystery. Even if my friends wouldn't like her—it seemed like *other* people would. If Jennifer made new friends, then we could hang out sometimes in our neighborhood, but stay separate at school.

I spent the first few hours of the day worried she'd say something to blow it, so I listened closely as the rumors about her swirled. Thankfully, it didn't seem like she'd mentioned anything about aliens, and I felt kinda good about that. Like I'd done something right. My advice helped her navigate seventh grade.

I waved and smiled at her in the hallways, but we didn't have any classes together, so I was in the clear.

Everything was going well, really—until lunchtime.

Reagan, Tess, and I were sitting at our lunch table in the corner, by the biggest cafeteria window.

"Well, I'm practically a whole new person after this summer," Reagan was saying, with mock seriousness. "For one thing, I discovered boobs, and that's been a game changer."

She was referencing the fact that her sister bought her a push-up bra, but that wasn't the only difference. Reagan had also come home with a new haircut: bangs that just brushed her eyelashes, which were thick with mascara. She looked so much older.

She waved her hands over her chest. "Behold," she announced, not loud enough for the other tables to hear her, but loud enough to make Tess and me blush. "The boobs have arrived."

I laughed, though I was now worrying about my own chest being too small.

Tess covered her face. "I can't deal with you." But she was laughing and glowing like people often glowed around Reagan. She made everyone brighter.

Reagan turned to me, eyes sparking. "And as for the second thing . . . this can't get out because I could get in a lot of trouble."

Instinctively, I bobbed my head, and I felt a shimmery bubble forming—just the two of us, protected from the outside world. She'd only just returned from her summer trip, and this was the first time I'd seen her in a whole month. Being with Jennifer made me feel raw, like I was exposed to all the questions in the universe. Being with Reagan made me feel safe.

"You know I'd never tell?" Tess said, popping my Mal-Reagan bubble. Her question-marking did not inspire confidence. Neither did the fact that she'd once admitted to "having a gossip problem."

Reagan continued, unfazed, "While I was staying with my sister, I learned how to drive."

"You drove?" Tess's eyes widened.

"Not just drove. Like, everyone can drive around a parking lot. But I drove constantly. I drove everywhere."

"And you didn't get caught?" I asked, hating that I sounded like a Goody Two-shoes.

Reagan grinned at me and I felt my heart hiccup. "You only get caught if you make a mistake," she said. "And I never do."

Tess twirled a curl. "And your sister let you?"

"My sister hates driving, so it worked out for everyone. Maybe if you two play your cards right, I can take you for a—"

"Pause, pause, pause," Tess interrupted. "Look who's here. Should we ask her to sit with us?"

I turned to see Jennifer, walking up to the lunch line. I bit my lip.

Reagan's brows pinched in annoyance. Just for a millisecond. Then they smoothed and she shrugged. "Honestly, who cares about the new girl?"

"You're right." Tess nodded, rearranging her expression from excitement to disgust. "I just think she's creepy? Like . . . what about the thing where she killed that kid back at her old school?"

If I'd had any hope of my friends liking Jennifer, it was gone now.

Reagan rolled her eyes. "Why is everyone so *morbid*?"

"That's not even the rumor," I said. "People are saying that about her *mom*." Pretty immediately, I realized that wasn't the right response.

Tess snorted. "Like mother, like daughter? Maybe they have mother-daughter murder sprees? To bond?" Then she gasped. "Oh, sorry, Reagan. I didn't mean to upset you?"

I hated when Tess did this—we'd be having a conversation about something totally separate, and then she'd pause to push one of Reagan's weak spots. It's like Tess was testing her for cracks.

Reagan met my eyes for an extra-long second before fake-smiling at Tess. "Why are you sorry, Tess? My mom wasn't murdered. She was struck by lightning. So I'm not sure why I'd be offended."

Tess laughed, kinda nervously. She pushed, sure, but at least she backed down before things went too far. "But what do you guys think about the new girl?" she asked, steering the conversation back toward safer ground. Toward Jennifer.

Reagan stared at me. She wasn't smiling this time, and I could see her hurt, hidden in the way her jaw muscle twitched, just barely. "Why don't you ask Mal? She met Jennifer this summer, after all."

"You *met* her?" Tess asked. "How? Did you guys hang out?"

With their eyes on me, I started to feel uncomfortable. These were my best friends. They expected me to tell them stuff. They trusted me. But so did Jennifer.

And suddenly I was frustrated, because I *knew* this would

79

happen. I never wanted to be in the middle, but here I was, and I hadn't *asked* for any of it.

"Only a little," I responded. "She didn't kill anyone. And neither did her mom."

"But how do you *know*?" Tess pushed. "Do you have some kind of secret connection?"

"What? No. It's not like that."

"Yeah, but you guys are similar? Like, obviously?"

I didn't know what Tess meant by that, which made me feel weird. Everything about Jennifer felt so opposite of me, but *were* we similar somehow? I felt like I had something in my teeth—obvious to everyone else, but I couldn't see it. I wrapped my arms around myself.

Reagan rolled her eyes. "Mal and her mom gave Jennifer a pie, and they all bonded. They're practically best friends now, and Mal's gonna leave her poor old friends behind, aren't you, Mal?"

I forced a laugh. "Definitely not best friends. But, just, you can't believe everything you hear, I guess."

"No . . . ," Reagan said slowly. Her eyes flashed. Shark Eyes. "You can't. But your new best friend is standing alone over there. Don't you want to say hi?"

She tilted her chin, gesturing across the cafeteria to where Jennifer stood with her tray and stared at the clusters of kids in front of her. She looked lost.

"Reagan," I said. Not as a warning, exactly, but a request. *Don't do it. Don't make this hard.*

Reagan looked past me and lifted her arm, waving. "Jennifer! Jennifer Chan!"

Jennifer jumped a bit, her eyes scanning the cafeteria until they landed on Reagan. Then me. Her face softened with relief.

My stomach flipped. "Reagan," I hissed. "Stop."

But my best friend ignored me.

Jennifer walked over to us and Reagan smiled—bright white, never-needed-braces perfection—all for the new girl. A part of me wanted to grab Reagan and pull her attention back to me.

"Jennifer!" Reagan beamed. "Aren't you just the cutest little celebrity today?"

Jennifer paused, looking at me. It took me a moment to realize she was waiting for me to say something. "Hi," I said, trying not to look at Tess, whose eyebrows went all the way up as she bit her metal straw.

I didn't know why Reagan had called Jennifer over. Maybe Reagan really did just want to meet her. But it felt cataclysmic, like planets colliding.

I cleared my throat and asked Jennifer, "Have you met Ingrid and Kath? I think you'd like them. They're sitting over there."

I pointed them out on the other side of the cafeteria.

Tess clarified, "That blond girl in blue, and the Black girl in the army jacket?"

Jennifer would get along with them much better than she would with my friends, and I felt a burst of relief, like I'd helped her and solved this messy friendship problem all at once.

Jennifer stood frozen, holding her tray, looking back and

forth between me and Kath and Ingrid, eyes dancing with confusion. But before she could respond, Reagan snorted.

"Don't be ridiculous," she said to Tess and me. To Jennifer, she gestured at the empty space beside me. "Sit."

Jennifer hesitated before sitting. I felt her looking at me again, but I just focused on my school lunch, nudging the brussels sprouts aside and spooning mashed potatoes into my mouth like they were the most delicious thing in the universe.

After a few beats of silence, Jennifer said, "I'm glad you called me over. Everybody already knows where they belong, and I didn't know where to go."

I wished she wouldn't admit that. It was too . . . much.

But Reagan nodded. "I was new here, too, last year."

Jennifer brightened, her caution slipping away. "I'm glad I'm not the only one!"

"We can show you around." Reagan actually looked genuine, and I started to feel that hope-flutter, like maybe this would all be okay. Like I could be friends with everyone, and nothing would be complicated. "So," Reagan added, folding her hands under her chin and raising her brows. "I hear you and Mallory bonded over the summer."

Jennifer nodded. "Oh yeah, we spent a lot of time together."

Reagan turned to me—and, like, could anyone else ever see her Shark Eyes? Was I the only one? "And yet Mallory has told me *none* of that. Because she's a bad friend." Reagan laughed at her joke.

I felt like I was gonna puke into my potatoes.

Jennifer smiled uncertainly. "Yeah, I actually taught her a lot about ali—"

"We didn't spend *that* much time together," I said quickly.

Jennifer frowned, and I watched as caution settled back over her. I felt panicked, and *frustrated* because I didn't want this to be a thing. Jennifer was gonna make it a thing and that was gonna be weird and I just wanted her to *get it*.

"I mean . . . ," Jennifer said slowly.

I tried to send her a message with my eyes, the way I always did with Reagan. *It's fine. Don't turn this into a big deal. Don't talk about aliens.*

But either Jennifer didn't understand, or she didn't care. "We did, though."

Silence stretched around us. I stared at those mashed potatoes as I searched for something to say, but I couldn't find it. I wished Reagan would make a joke, save me, anything.

Tess smacked her lips. "Awwwkward."

I kind of wanted to throw a brussels sprout right at Tess's face.

Jennifer ignored her and looked at me. "Why are you acting like this?"

My mouth went dry. Jennifer had no sense of what she should say and what she shouldn't. Who sits down at a new school, with a group of girls who just so happen to be the popular girls, and starts a whole *thing*?

"Acting like what?" I managed.

With her looking at me like that, I felt a little bad. But I wasn't *doing* anything. I wasn't the one coming in here, confronting someone in front of their friends, making things totally weird and awkward.

Quietly, she said, "Acting like you barely know me."

"Well, I've only known you for a few weeks. . . ."

Tess made a little *ohhh* sound.

I hadn't meant to sound mean. I really, really hadn't. It was just *true*. Only it did sound kind of mean.

I wanted to reel the words back in, but they were already out, and what then? What was I supposed to do?

Reagan looked at me like she was searching for the truth. And in that moment I wished I didn't know her quite so well. I wished I couldn't see the hurt beneath her blank expression—like she believed I'd leave her, and she was simply waiting for me to prove her right.

"I mean . . . it's not like . . . ," I stammered. But guilt settled in my stomach, churning with those mashed potatoes, and I couldn't finish the sentence. Turning to Jennifer for as long as I could bear, I whispered, "I'm sorry."

It was like Jennifer hadn't even heard me. "Oh," she said flatly. "I get it." That girl I'd met this summer, with so much spark and hope, wasn't there anymore.

She grabbed her tray and stood. "You're mean girls."

It was too loud in the cafeteria for other kids to hear our conversation, but people glanced over as Jennifer stood. Our classmates watched as she walked away from us and toward Kath and Ingrid. People noted the look on Jennifer's face—and the looks on ours.

She had taken a giant spotlight and shined it right on us, and none of us were ready. I felt ill.

Reagan blinked. "Mean girls?"

Tess laughed, like none of this mattered, but Reagan just looked at me, eyes wide, confused. "I was trying to be nice," she said. "Like, literally, I was being nice."

"I know," I said. And she *was*. I'm pretty sure she was. I still felt dizzy, trying to figure out what just happened.

"God, she, like, walked up here, talked to us for two minutes, and judged us based on nothing," Reagan said.

And maybe Reagan was right. Maybe Jennifer should have given them more of a chance. Maybe then everything would have been different.

Reagan shook her head and said slowly, full of ice, "Who does she think she is?"

Now

12

The next morning, I'm having trouble focusing at our weekly grade-wide assembly. We're all packed into the chapel, with those hard-back pews, and Principal Vaughn is giving the same speech he gives every week, about teamwork and industrious spirit—but how can we think about anything except the last time we were in here? How can we think about anything but Jennifer?

Next to me, Tess whispers something, but I can't bring myself to pay attention to that, either. Reagan's somewhere behind us, sitting in the back of the chapel with Pete. And despite everything else that's happening, I'm still kind of upset about that, because friends don't ditch each other, not even for a crush. I don't know if she's avoiding me after I asked her about finding Jennifer yesterday—or if she just doesn't care. But I don't understand how my friends can be so uninterested, how they aren't more *worried*.

For the first time, I wonder if my friends are good people. And I wonder if I am. Would I have helped if the situation were reversed? If I'd barely known Jennifer, and Kath approached me?

The assembly is nearly over when Principal Vaughn clears his throat and straightens his tie, always a sign that he's going off script. The microphone screeches briefly, and we all wince. "Many of you have come to me with questions and concerns, and I know you are scared. This is a difficult time. But I've also been moved by the outpouring of love. I'm reminded, like I so often am, of how much we support one another here at Gibbons Academy, and in Norwell."

Principal Vaughn has talked like this about our school and about Nowhereville before, about how we're all one big family, full of small-town spirit and love. He seems to genuinely believe it, but when I look around, I don't see it. I wonder if something's missing in this place, or if something's missing in me.

"And I assure you that the police are working very hard," he continues. "This is a time to trust the experts, and it's very important to tell them everything you know. If anybody has any information, please come forward."

My heart squeezes. In my imagination, the whole grade turns to look at me. In reality, no one's looking.

I'm supposed to trust the adults, tell them what I know— but I don't *know* anything. And the stuff I think, well, I can't come forward with it. Nobody would listen, nobody would believe in *aliens*. And if people found out about the Incident . . . But no. That's irrelevant.

If Jennifer left because of aliens, then the Incident doesn't actually matter. It was all just a coincidence. Telling anyone about that would just get my friends and me in trouble. It would *distract* from finding Jennifer.

Right?

The ringing in my ears transforms into a single word. *Tell, tell, tell.* It screams over the thump of my heart. *Don't, don't, don't.*

In an act of desperation, I look to the ceiling of the chapel and think, *What should I do? Tell me what to do.*

I don't know who I'm asking—God or aliens or myself or what—but of course nobody answers.

I feel faint.

Then the microphone feedback screeches again, and we all jump in our seats. Only this time, instead of fading away, the sound changes to static.

And then there's a loud beep. It's so loud that everyone's hands fly to their ears. Students look around, bug-eyed. Some kids laugh.

But something echoes in my memory, and my eyes dart toward the clock. I start to count the seconds.

Principal Vaughn scrambles to switch off the podium microphone, but the sound continues. He signals to the media tech room in the back of the chapel, trying to catch the audio tech teacher's attention, as if she hasn't already noticed the earsplitting sound.

Thirty-five seconds.

"Make it stop!" a boy groans from the back, miming death-by-annoying-noise as he slides off his pew. His friends laugh.

Fifty-five seconds.

There have been technical difficulties during assemblies before, but they've never lasted so long. And they've never been so loud.

Our principal attempts to shout over the noise. "Sorry for the interruption. Not to worry!"

The seconds on the clock spill over a minute, ticking by. Sixty-five. Seventy. Seventy-one. Seventy-two.

And then, finally, the sound stops.

My ears ring in the absence of noise, and goose bumps skitter up my spine. Seventy-two seconds. The length of the *Wow!* signal.

I scan the chapel and meet Kath's eyes. She turns and whispers something to Ingrid, who stiffens.

The silence is filled with the sound of eighty students talking, and Principal Vaughn has to shout to get our attention. "Quiet! Quiet, please."

It only kind of works. We are quiet*er,* but still murmuring. It's like we're all bottles of pent-up nerves after Jennifer ran, and this has set us loose. Next to me, Tess says, "So weird."

Giving up on order, Principal Vaughn says, "Assembly dismissed. Please *calmly* make your way to your next period."

Everyone stands and shuffles out, their conversations merging into a single buzz. Among the mass of my classmates, Tess and I search for Reagan, but I catch only a glimpse of her before Pete blocks her from view.

We're nearly out of the chapel when I spot Ingrid again. She's shouldering past the crowd, with Kath trailing behind her.

"Was that what Kath thinks it was?" Ingrid asks when she

reaches us. Her tone is cautious, but there's that unmistakable lilt of curiosity beneath it, and I can't stop the hope that catches in my chest.

Beside me, Tess asks, "Um, what are you talking about?"

When Ingrid ignores her, Tess raises a brow and pushes, like she always does. "Mal, do *you* know what Ingrid's talking about?"

"Wow," I murmur.

Tess frowns. "Wow, *what*?"

Seeing the curl of disgust on her lips, I feel a hot flash of embarrassment—and then the shame that follows. I hate that there's a part of me that doesn't want to be seen talking to Kath and Ingrid.

I don't even care what Tess thinks, or at least I don't *want* to care, but that feeling's still there—like everyone's watching and judging me. I want to crawl right out of my skin, but I inhale, exhale. *Deep breaths, Mallory.*

"I want to talk to Kath and Ingrid," I tell Tess.

Tess laughs, like I must be joking. "Why?"

Kath rolls her eyes. "Because we are delightful, Tess. It's not rocket science."

Tess sputters in shock, and I struggle to bury my laugh.

Borrowing some of Kath's confidence for myself, I tell Tess, "Just . . . go. Go."

Her eyes narrow, and I get the neck-prickling sense that she'll make me regret that. Then she spins on her heel and walks away.

As soon as she's gone, Ingrid asks me, "Did you cause that signal?"

I shake my head, but it's Kath who answers, voice low. "She couldn't have. The only way to do that is through the chapel's audio system, which is in the locked media tech room."

Ingrid and I follow her gaze to the small room at the back of the chapel, where all the sound tech is housed, as well as the broadcast system used for school-wide announcements. I know, vaguely, that the Audio Tech Club handles the lights and sound for chapel performances, and that they do morning announcements, but I've never given the sound system much thought.

"Most kids don't have access to the media tech room without a teacher present," Kath continues. "And only a handful of people know the key code: me, since I'm the Audio Tech Club president; the chaplains; our club supervisor, Ms. Lucas; and our club VP, Kyle."

We turn toward Kyle, who's standing on the other side of the chapel with Pete, Reagan, and now Tess. He's laughing and doing a flailing version of some TikTok dance.

"Maybe he did it to interrupt the assembly?" Ingrid suggests. "So we'd get out early?"

Kath shakes her head. "He might *want* to do that, but he's as smart as a bag of rocks. He would've had to set the signal earlier today, and he'd have to code it to override the system so Principal Vaughn and Ms. Lucas couldn't just turn it off. Kyle's only doing media production for club credit. He has no idea how to work the equipment."

"So, the teachers have no reason to hack the assembly. And if it wasn't a student . . ." I lower my voice. "Could it actually be . . ."

91

"Aliens?" Ingrid finishes, looking skeptical.

"Wow," I say.

Kat hesitates, looking a little sick. Then she nods. "Wow."

"We still don't know anything for sure." Ingrid exhales, long and slow. "But . . . I'm intrigued."

I'm torn between fainting and cheering. How are you supposed to feel when you've been contacted by aliens? How are you supposed to feel when the two smartest kids in the grade might help you find them? *Be cool, be cool.*

"So, Ingrid . . . ," I begin. Kath and I exchange a glance, trying to contain our excitement. "Are you in?"

Ingrid turns to Kath, who looks so star-bright hopeful that Ingrid can't help but grin. As soon as I see her smile, I can't help it, either.

Things might have changed, but the Ingrid who needs answers is still in there.

"Something's definitely going on here," she says. "So how could I possibly say no?"

Jennifer Chan's Guide to the Universe
Volume V, Entry No. 21: What I Need

Dad's too sick to search for aliens now, so it's all up to me.

"Look for those three flashes," he said to me a few days ago, when I was trying not to cry, "and you'll know there's something up there, watching out for you."

I've slept in my tent outside every night since, even though Rebecca doesn't like it. She tried to camp out with me one of those nights, but I told her no. It's me and Dad's thing.

It's hard to do it alone, of course, because the world is easier with someone who gets you. But if I <u>have</u> to do it alone, I can do it for him, and for me. I have my research, and my courage, and my strength. And that's everything I'm ever going to need.

Now

13

Kath, Ingrid, and I text our parents during lunch, telling them we have a project to work on, so Kath and Ingrid are allowed to come over after school. We still don't have a plan, but with Ingrid involved, we have hope.

Mom picks us up, and when we all pile into the car, the feeling of Mom picking my friends and me up from school is so déjà vu that I feel disoriented. This should be Reagan here. But it's not.

With Mom watching us, the tension between Kath, Ingrid, and me amplifies. All the extraterrestrial excitement has distracted us from the weirdness of not necessarily liking each other. But now, as the whole car fills with silence, we can't avoid it.

Mom makes eye contact with me in the rearview mirror, and I can see all the questions she's dying to ask. When I texted her about Kath and Ingrid, she pelted me with *What project? Did you choose your own partners? Are you and Ingrid friends again?*

I shake my head at her, just slightly. *Mom, don't.*

"Hi, girls," she says in the most normal voice she can muster. She turns the radio down a little and beams. "It's great to see you again, Ingrid. And, Kath, it's so nice to meet you."

Ingrid says hello, and Kath starts asking Mom about work—about the state of the college and the *administration*. Both my parents work at a college, but I've never even thought to ask about the administration. It makes me feel kind of weird that Kath's known Mom for about two seconds and they already get along better than I do with either of them.

I turn to my phone and send a group text to Kath and Ingrid. It's the first time I've texted either of them.

We should think about our first step.

But Kath's still talking to Mom, and Ingrid's still nodding along politely. Neither of them even checks their phone. Reagan and I used to text the whole car ride, but I remind myself: things are different now.

Mom looks back at me, and I know she's about to ask all her questions.

Mom, no. No, no, no.

She opens her mouth, expression all innocence.

But suddenly the deep voice of our local radio host turns to static. Ingrid, Kath, and I exchange wide-eyed glances as Mom fiddles with the buttons, trying to find a station that will play anything other than static.

And then we hear a series of beeps. Not one long sound, but short bursts, no matter what station Mom turns to. It's loud, nearly rattling the car. The sound reaches right into my brain and shakes it.

"This is so strange," Mom says, bringing a hand to her forehead, pinching between her eyebrows. Static. A headache. More signs that Jennifer mentioned.

When I turn to Kath and Ingrid, I can practically see the exclamation points in their eyes. I filled them in on the alien signs while we waited for Mom, and now they're putting the pieces together.

Chills run up my arms. First it was just me, witnessing the UAP. Then it was the school. Now it's the local radio—encompassing the whole town.

This makes aliens feel so real, so close—but fear starts to whisper in my ear. *I might be in over my head.*

I shake my shoulders, pushing the worry away. Then I gesture to my phone, trying to convey to Kath and Ingrid that we should discuss this over text.

They don't get the hint.

Ingrid says, "Was that—"

"Are you all right, Mrs. Moss?" Kath interrupts, shooting Ingrid a *Be chill!* look.

Mom takes a deep breath. "Yeah, sorry about that. That static just gave me an awful headache."

Kath turns to us. "This just got more interesting," she murmurs.

Mom rubs her forehead as the local station blips back on. A male voice rumbles on about climate change as if nothing extraordinary just happened.

"Must have been some kind of glitch," Mom says.

I nod. But Ingrid, Kath, and I know better.

The three of us contain ourselves until we get to my room, and then we burst, questions and excitement and panic spilling out.

Kath shakes her head, eyes wide. "Is it real? I mean, is it possible? Could this alien stuff be *real*?"

I pace in front of my bed because I can't possibly sit still. "You heard the sound system at school today."

"Well, yeah, but this is . . ." Kath chews her cheek. "This was different from school. This was . . ."

"Bigger," I finish. "I agree. And it was exactly how Jennifer described it. The static, the beeps, even a headache."

Ingrid's wired, all her muscles vibrating with tension. Her foot tap-tap-taps at top speed, keeping pace with her racing brain. "Okay. Let's work out what we know."

I start with the obvious. "We know that aliens are communicating over the radio."

"We know that *something* is happening over the radio," Ingrid corrects.

Kath leans forward. "Something that sounds a lot like Jennifer's aliens."

I mouth a *thanks* at Kath, still surprised she believes. She shrugs.

"Okay. Okay, okay, okay. I did some research during free period this afternoon." Ingrid pauses, as if she's expecting us to stop her. When we don't, she continues. "As I see it, there are three major obstacles."

She takes a spiral notebook off my desk and tears out three blank sheets of paper. I wince at the ripping sound.

"Sorry," Ingrid says, noting my reaction. "I forgot you're the type who doesn't like to mess up your stuff. Your desk is pretty pristine."

When she says it, I see my room through her eyes. White walls, white desk, white comforter. Everything in its place. Mom's always suggesting I add "statement pieces," but I don't like loud statements.

"It's fine," I say.

"Ingrid's just used to her own room," Kath says, "which is utter chaos."

"*Organized* chaos," Ingrid insists.

"Still chaos."

Ingrid flashes Kath a grin and grabs one of my pens. Then she writes one word on each paper: *MALAISE, METHOD,* and *MESSAGE.*

Kath raises a brow. "*Malaise?*"

"It means 'a bad feeling,' " Ingrid explains.

Malaise sounds much worse than "bad feeling," and that uneasiness curdles in my chest. I ignore it.

"Let's start with that, then," Ingrid says, pointing to the *Malaise* paper. "What are our concerns about safety and negative consequences?"

"Principal Vaughn told us to trust the experts. If we look for aliens on our own, we aren't doing that," Kath says. "And we're going against the police, too. Which is dangerous."

The air in my room seems to thicken as the awareness between us grows: this is real, and our actions could have real consequences.

Ingrid adds, "And that's not even considering actually finding aliens. That could also be dangerous."

Her worry echoes my own, but then I remember something Jennifer said during one of her visits this summer. "Jennifer talked about aliens being altruistic. Like, if they managed to advance without killing each other, then they must be a peaceful species."

Ingrid grimaces. "Alternatively, what if one group of aliens killed all the others and then set off to colonize the rest of the universe? That's likely what humans would do, if we could."

I didn't consider that possibility. But I want to believe what Jennifer said. "Aliens might have been like that before, but they probably aren't *anymore*. They've probably evolved to be . . . nice to one another."

Ingrid raises her brows. "Do you think humans could ever evolve to be nice to one another?"

I don't know how to respond. I don't remember Ingrid being so cynical.

But Kath says, "It's possible, I think."

I'm realizing Kath is far more optimistic than I gave her credit for.

Ingrid recoils a little at Kath's response. "But do you think humans would ever care about other people, or other species, more than themselves?"

When Jennifer talked about this, she seemed so confident. It was easy to get swept up in it. But now I don't know.

"Maybe they'd care if they felt like they really could make a difference," I say. "And maybe the aliens know they can make a difference because they have better technology and more knowledge. They can really change things for us."

Ingrid takes a deep breath. "It's just a big ask . . . ," she says, "to believe in goodness."

Sympathy flashes across Kath's face, and again, I wonder what happened to make Ingrid so . . . hopeless.

"It's a risk," I say softly. "But if the aliens *are* dangerous, and Jennifer found them, that would mean . . ."

Quiet falls over us. None of us want to finish that thought.

Finally, Kath reaches past us and flips over *Malaise*. "We understand the risks, and we'll be as careful as possible."

I nod and point to the next paper. Nowhere to go but forward. "Now, what's *Method*?"

Ingrid shakes off her emotion and continues, all practical. "We need to consider the logistics of contact. Based on my research, it seems like most scientists in the SETI Institute—the Search for Extraterrestrial Intelligence—believe the best way to reach aliens is either with radio waves or giant lasers.

Radio is obviously gonna be easier for us. But astronomers use giant radio telescopes—basically huge satellite dishes."

"The Big Ear," I say.

Ingrid nods. "If we had one that could send and receive signals, we might be able to make contact."

"But we don't have one of those," Kath reminds us.

"They probably have those at the military base," I say.

Kath frowns. "And we *definitely* can't get one from there."

Ingrid blinks. "Why not?"

"What, three kids are going to break into a *military base*?"

Ingrid looks like she's actually calculating the possibility. "I guess my mom was pretty mad when Mallory and I set that fire at Howard Park. She was upset that we were *near* a base, because she said if a military person found us, we would have gotten into way more trouble."

"To be fair," I say, "she wasn't *just* mad that we were near the base. She was also mad about the literal fire."

"True."

Kath looks at us like we've lost our minds. "Can we all agree that we're *not* going to break into a military base? Or set fire to anything?"

Reluctantly, Ingrid nods.

"Yes," I say. "But what about the local radio station?"

Kath rubs her temples. "That could work. But again, that would mean breaking and entering. Even if we wanted to, there'd be too much security."

I tap my fingers against my thigh as we consider the possibilities—and the impossibilities. "What about a car radio?" I suggest. "We know it responds to . . . whatever's happening."

Ingrid shakes her head. "We need two-way communication if we're going to ask them about Jennifer."

Kath leans forward. "I think my dad has some old walkie-talkies in our garage. He never throws stuff out."

"That's not strong enough," Ingrid says.

"They're long-range walkies."

"Long enough for *space*?"

Kath pauses. "Touché."

We're silent as we think. It's frustrating. There are ways to make contact, but we don't have access to any of them. What if aliens really are here, and they have Jennifer, and there's nothing we can do about it?

"Or . . . ," I say, an idea forming. "What about the media tech room in the chapel? They definitely have the technology to send and receive a signal. Input and output."

Ingrid's eyes widen. "That's perfect. *And* we could do some investigating into the assembly signal. There might be clues about what caused it."

Both Ingrid and I turn to Kath, who balks. "We're only supposed to use the equipment for school-related activities," she says.

"Jennifer's a student at our school," I say, "so *technically* it is school-related."

"*Technically* it's not."

It's Ingrid's turn to make star-bright hope eyes. "The chapel's always open, but nobody's ever there during lunch.

We could slip in quickly. And, Kath . . . you have the key code."

"I could get in a lot of trouble. . . ." Kath bites her cuticles, a nervous habit.

"Please," I beg. "It's for Jennifer."

Kath closes her eyes, debating. Then she sighs. "You're right. This is more important than the rules. We can go during lunch tomorrow."

I do an internal happy dance, then lean over and flip the *Method* page so it's just a blank sheet. "Second problem: solved."

Ingrid points to the last paper. "So, *Message*. If we're going to send a message, we need to tune the radio to the right frequency. There are tons of channels, and it's unlikely that aliens are monitoring every single one."

"Jennifer talked about finding the right number to dial," I say. "Is that what she meant?"

"It sounds like it." Ingrid frowns. "But I wouldn't even know where to start."

"Jennifer's done *years* of research, and we don't have time to catch up," I say. And then an idea begins to buzz in my chest. "Unless . . . we use her research."

They both look at me, and I push back my doubts. "I know where she kept all that research. She had these journals. . . ."

Mentioning the journals makes my hands shake, so I stuff them into my pockets. "She kept them in her bedroom. We could get all of them." That's a lie. We wouldn't get all of them. But I don't want to tell them about Volume VII, the journal Jennifer pressed into my palms the first day I met her. We don't need to talk about that.

Kath stares. "So, somehow we've returned to breaking and entering?"

Ingrid and I exchange a glance. There's that spark of a challenge in her eyes. Because compared to a radio station or a military base . . . sneaking into Jennifer's room doesn't seem impossible.

Kath looks back and forth between us. "Do all your plans involve literal *crime*?"

"It's like you said," I explain. "This is more important than rules."

"I was talking about *school rules*. Not the *actual law*," Kath sputters. "You're talking about breaking into the home of a missing girl. Do you realize how suspicious that looks?"

I hesitate. Kath's right. "But . . . we can't find Jennifer if we can't find the right frequency," I say. "And we have to find her."

Kath looks like she might pass out. "I understand that. But you can't just . . ." She pauses as Ingrid and I exchange another glance. Kath folds her arms over her chest. "Stop looking at each other like that."

"Like what?" I ask.

"Like you're *scheming*."

Ingrid laughs, and I realize that I haven't heard her laugh in over a year.

And then Kath adds, "Like you're . . . friends."

Ingrid's laugh cuts off, swallowed back. That shimmery

excitement evaporates, and we realize we aren't friends planning an adventure. This is a temporary truce.

"I think there are two options," I say. "Number one: you could sleep over tonight. I overheard my parents talking about the search, and they said Ms. Chan's been leaving at five every morning to look for Jennifer. After she leaves, the house will be empty, and we'll have an hour-long window before my parents wake up. And we shouldn't have a problem getting in, because Ms. Chan always leaves the door unlocked for Jennifer, just in case. . . ."

We all wince as we think of Jennifer, out there somewhere, far from home.

"Or option two," I continue. "I can do it myself. You're both right. There are risks, with aliens and with breaking in. You don't have to get involved."

It's almost physically painful to say, and the thought of doing this alone turns my panic into a black hole. But as much as I want their help, I don't want to get them into trouble.

Kath and Ingrid share a silent conversation, and as I watch them, I wish I could understand their secret, best friend language.

Then Kath sighs as she flips over the *Message* paper. "Oh, come on. Let's contact some aliens."

Then
15

After the unfortunate cafeteria interaction on the first day of school, things got worse for Jennifer. Once Reagan and Tess rejected her, her newness tipped in the opposite direction: Jennifer was no longer the cool, mysterious new girl. She was the weird, awkward new girl.

Pete, Kyle, and the rest of that group didn't wait long to start mocking her, after that. Within a week, they were doing karate chops and martial arts kicks as she passed in the hallway, before cracking up as if they'd achieved record levels of comedy.

Eventually, all that led to the infamous kung fu face-off.

It's not like it was planned, necessarily. Or at least, if it was planned, I had no idea. But when I got to school that morning, the air was crackling with a sharp, sour energy.

It was half an hour before the first bell, but already, a crowd had gathered around the benches near the front of the school. As usual, Pete, Kyle, and all their friends were hanging out there, but unlike usual, they were alert, more awake at this hour than they should have been. They were ready. Waiting.

Everything felt *off*. The sign by the school drop-off, warning us that the sheriff was always watching, felt ominous instead of comforting. The lovebugs had started to appear, and they flitted past, threatening to tangle in my hair. The air was climbing to a temperature that made me want to leave my body.

I pushed past the crowd of my classmates, past noise, laughter, fear, and disapproval all rolled together—until I found Reagan. She was alone because Tess was late that morning, and she was standing near the back of the crowd.

"What's happening?" I asked.

"The whole karate thing." She swatted at a lovebug and sighed like she was bored, but something dark flashed in her eyes. Anticipation. "Pete's waiting for Jennifer."

A stress headache bloomed behind my brows. "What's he gonna do? Should we stop him? Should we say something?"

Reagan shot me a look, annoyed and a little hurt. "She'll be fine."

And then, as if Reagan had summoned her, Jennifer appeared.

Or at least, that's how I remember it. A weird thing happens when you see something with your own eyes and then you hear about it later. It's like your reality merges with the rumors, and you aren't sure what's real anymore. You can't trust your own memory.

But here's what I remember:

Jennifer walked up and looked at the crowd, confused, interested, trying to figure out what everyone was waiting for. As soon as she approached, Pete stood slowly, stretching his long limbs. "Hey there, Jennifer Chan," he said, enunciating each syllable of her name. He stuck his hands into his pockets and grinned.

I'd seen that smile before. He used it on Reagan sometimes, and I didn't trust it. I didn't trust *Pete*. He acted like everything was a game, like he could hurt people without caring about the consequences.

I bit my lip so hard it hurt. *Jennifer, get out of here.*

Jennifer frowned and I could see her piecing things together, slowly realizing that the crowd was there for her. She looked out at us. Then she looked at *me* and held my gaze just a little too long.

I looked down.

"What?" Jennifer asked Pete, her tone cautious.

He dialed up the charm, running his hand through his sandy-blond hair and grinning in a way that showed off his dimples. "You've been here for a whole week now, and you haven't properly introduced yourself."

This was wrong—this wouldn't end well. I looked around for a teacher, hoping hard that one might magically appear. But none of them did.

"Um, sorry?" Jennifer's voice shook a little, and for a second, I thought I could hear her heart pounding. But no, that was my own.

Even more kids now, and maybe some of them were on

the verge of stepping in, gritting their teeth and praying things wouldn't get too bad.

But some kids wanted a show. And deep down, I worried I was one of them. I knew I wasn't, mostly. But it was hard to know myself one hundred percent. It was hard to be sure there wasn't a scrap of me that wanted something exciting to happen.

I shivered.

A few people lifted their phones to film the scene. Reagan crossed her arms over her chest and held so still she barely seemed to breathe.

Jennifer wince-smiled, a polite kind of fear, and tried to step around Pete.

His friends blocked her. The other kids surrounded her. She was trapped.

"Jennifer, you've been ignoring me," Pete said, all dimples and fake hurt. "Now you've got to make that up to me."

Jennifer's smile faltered. She glanced around at the crowd. There must have been a part of her that screamed *Run away!*

But something flickered in her eyes—a flash of fear, and then a softening. I watched her make the decision to trust him.

I wanted to scream, I wanted to stop this, but there was nothing I could do.

"What do you want me to do?" she asked.

It was like he'd set a giant trap and she'd looked at it and said, *That's a very nice trap! Can I hang out in it?*

Pete looked down to hide a smirk. He kicked at the concrete with his shoe, acting embarrassed. When he looked back up, his expression was all nervous and trusting—a mirror of Jennifer's.

It looked real. That's what was scary.

"Maaaybe," he said, dragging the word out, "you could show me some of your kung fu moves? It's just—I've heard so much about your kung fu, but I've never actually seen you do it."

Someone coughed to cover up a laugh.

I locked eyes with Reagan, and she shook her head ever so slightly. *Don't get involved.*

We all knew what was happening. Jennifer's karate thing was just a little too weird for Nowhereville, and if she did it here, in front of everyone, that would give people more fuel to make fun of her.

I swallowed. I wanted to stop it, but panic had reached up and wrapped its hand around my throat. I couldn't move. I couldn't help her.

I wished I could make a difference, but Pete was way more popular than me, so I knew he wouldn't listen.

The only thing that made me feel better was knowing that Pete burned through his mockery quickly. He'd spend a week or so focusing on one person, before getting bored and moving on. As long as she let this blow over, Jennifer would be okay.

"It's called capoeira, actually," she said. She looked at the crowd, and the worst part of all was the expression on her face. That freaking hopeful expression.

She had to know—she *had to know*—that they were

making fun of her. But maybe she wanted it to be real so badly that she ignored that little detail. "It's a Brazilian form of martial arts. My dad used to practice with me before he died."

At her blunt, matter-of-fact way of speaking about death, Pete seemed to hesitate. That fake-friendly act faltered, replaced by a flicker of something genuine.

But the flicker blew out quickly, and then he was back to normal. "Show me? Please with a pretty cherry?"

At the familiar phrase, I looked at Reagan. Her eyes narrowed and she took a deep breath. I couldn't tell if she was pleased or annoyed, and that shook me. I'd grown so fluent in her language, and not understanding her was unsettling.

I turned back to Jennifer and watched. We all watched.

Jennifer grinned, like no matter how tense the situation, capoeira was something she couldn't resist. "Okay, if you're really interested."

She bent over and rocked from foot to foot, swinging her arms in front of her.

Cough-laughter rippled through the crowd.

Mom would have been so disappointed. She would have told me to march through the crowd, waving my arms, shouting, *Neither karate nor capoeira is embarrassing! It is impressive, and you should all be ashamed of yourselves!*

But I'm not like that.

Then Jennifer did a spinning kick.

And it *was* impressive, actually. The crowd sounded like static—a mix of laughter and whispers and then, too, *wows*.

Nobody knew how to react, so they looked to Pete and Reagan.

Reagan rolled her eyes.

But Pete's whole face changed. He leaned forward, his expression sliding from mocking to interest. "That was cool," he said.

Jennifer met his gaze. "I know."

"Can you do another one?"

Her hands weren't shaking anymore. The kick had steadied her. She looked at Pete, and then at the crowd, frowning as if she were coming out of a daze, as if she were seeing their laughter and phones for the first time. "I'm not gonna do tricks for you. I'm not a puppy."

It's basically impossible to get a crowd of amped-up middle schoolers to go silent. But Jennifer did the impossible. Because the surprising thing wasn't *what* she said. It was *how* she said it. Not tough, like those words might be, but almost kindly, like she was explaining something important to him. Something he just didn't get.

I felt a rush of fear and worry, and then also . . . pride. Because Pete always did this kind of thing to people, but nobody ever reacted like *that*.

It was awesome.

Other people must have felt it, too, because some of the girls laughed. *With* her, this time, instead of at her.

Pete grinned, full on. This wasn't fake or calculated. Somehow, in just a few moments, Jennifer had changed what people thought of her. Somehow, Jennifer had won him over.

She had *won*.

Something loosened in my chest, and weirdly, I wanted to cry.

Then Pete nodded slowly, spoke even slower. "You're . . . different."

In the way that only Pete could, he sucked the oxygen out of the atmosphere. They were just two little words, but he said *different* as if he meant *better*, and it made me feel small.

The truth is, his words hurt, like an unexpected paper cut—a deep red slice that stings but doesn't bleed. And you can't complain, because it's just a paper cut. It's not that bad, really.

I stood there thinking, *I want to be different*.

And Reagan, I'm sure, thought, *I'm supposed to be different*.

I wondered if Pete knew what he'd just done—if boys used their words like weapons, too.

And I wondered if *Jennifer* knew what she'd just done. If she had somehow planned all this to seem different, to seem better.

Jennifer blinked at him, then at the crowd. We were all waiting for what she'd say next, and under everyone's gaze, she said simply, "I know."

Then she turned away from him and pushed through the crowd, refusing to make eye contact with anyone.

Reagan turned on her heel and walked in the opposite direction, and I stood frozen for a few seconds, not sure who to follow.

I caught up with Reagan eventually. But maybe if I'd followed Jennifer, none of this would have happened. Maybe I could have explained: *Hey, you're upsetting the popularity chain. Which isn't bad, of course, but maybe you shouldn't. If you keep acting like you're above it all, people will get mad. People like Reagan. And that would be bad.*

I told myself that was the key. Jennifer just needed to know how the world worked. And she needed somebody to tell her.

Jennifer Chan's Guide to the Universe
Volume V, Entry No. 48: Defense

Dad taught me capoeira. Not a whole lot. Just basic stuff. I didn't want to learn it at first, because I don't like violence or anything close to it. But then he taught me some history.

"Sometimes, the world tries to take things and strip them of their meaning," he said. "But remember: meaning is a gift."

He told me that capoeira is popular in Brazil, but it started long before that, in Africa. It started with people who were stolen from their homes and brought to a new land, where they were trapped and enslaved.

I'd learned about slavery in the US, but I hadn't realized it expanded globally—another example of all the horrifying things humans do to one another.

Some people debate the history of capoeira, but here's the dominant theory: It was an art back in Africa, a beautiful form of self-defense, practiced freely. But when Africans were enslaved in Brazil, they had to hide that defense in the form of dance. They had to disguise its power. They protected themselves with beauty.

And thinking about that gave me goose bumps all over. Because how did humans manage to make something so beautiful out of violence, while living under violence?

I'm still practicing capoeira, even though Dad's too weak to teach me anymore. And Mom's much happier about the capoeira than the alien search. She says self-defense is practical, that I need to prepare myself for how the real world works.

But learning about aliens is a form of self-defense, too. And maybe this sounds wild, but I've learned a lot about turning violence into beauty by researching alien conspiracies.

Take Area 51, for example. It started as a testing site for nuclear weapons, and the government planned to turn it into a dumping ground for nuclear waste.

Can you even imagine? The US was making so many nuclear weapons that they needed thousands of acres to bury all that leftover poison. That would make the land deadly for thousands of years.

Pretty terrible, if you ask me. I mean, the military wanted to destroy all these acres of land, basically forever, just so they could practice killing people. That's not a great look for humans.

You'd think humans would've learned something after whole centuries of war. You'd think they would've learned to avoid it.

That's what the aliens were probably thinking, too. Because weird things started happening in Area 51. People started seeing things that couldn't have possibly come from this world. Malfunctions started happening that couldn't possibly be coincidences. Like, one time during a nuclear test, just before twelve weapons were set to launch, every single one of them shut down. That shouldn't have happened. The weapon systems weren't linked. So maybe one might have failed, but not all of them.

Nobody at the military base could figure it out. But it seemed like someone—or something—had jammed the signal. Probably something extraterrestrial.

If you've been following along, you get it, right?

After war after war after war—after watching us hurt each other and the Earth, after seeing us on the brink of nuclear disaster—the aliens finally came to stop us.

They came to save us from ourselves.

And now? Area 51 isn't known for violence. Now it's a mysterious, magical place. It's a place people travel to see. It's a place people write about and dream about.

It's a place that makes people believe—for a lifetime or even for a moment—that impossible things are possible.

Now

16

Here's the plan: Kath will be our lookout, watching Jennifer's house from my living room window and texting us updates. I'll sneak into the house and grab Jennifer's journals. Ingrid will be waiting under Jennifer's window, and I'll toss the journals down to her. Then I'll sneak out, and we'll have all the research we need to find Jennifer.

Thankfully, our parents allowed them to sleep over, which is pretty lucky, considering it's a school night. I guess the three of us hanging out was so unlikely that our parents figured it must be for school.

Kath and Ingrid went home briefly to grab sleepover stuff, and then we spent the rest of the evening hashing out the plan.

Now they're asleep, but I'm finding sleep kind of impossible. I wake up every fifteen minutes because every little light outside could be a UFO. Every little sound could be Jennifer.

At 3 a.m., I give up on sleep and start Googling aliens. I scroll through famous extraterrestrial spots in the US—

Roswell and Area 51—and I wonder if Nowhereville might be on that list one day.

Google sends me from one link to the next, and an hour and a half later, I'm reading about stars. Some stars are solitary—a single bright spot in the pitch black of space. But some stars come in doubles. They orbit each other, passing so close that their star stuff flows between them.

It's strange to think of stars as something so fuzzy that their insides aren't even contained. Like, if they get close enough, it's no longer clear where one ends and the other begins.

The thought makes me jittery.

I turn off my phone and sit up. Then I tiptoe out of my bedroom. I don't have time to fall back asleep anyway.

From my living room, I watch Jennifer's house, waiting for her mom to leave, and I pace, pace, pace. I've gotten good at that lately. The problem is, pacing makes me think. And I start thinking that maybe I shouldn't have involved Kath and Ingrid. They've already helped a lot, but maybe they were right not to trust me. Maybe they shouldn't get close enough to share my star stuff.

I feel a black hole of worry growing, which might be the worst feeling in the world, and I'm starting to get that panic cloud again—

"*Pssst*," someone whispers into my ear, so close that their breath tickles the hairs on my neck.

I spin around, terror seizing my muscles. My brain short-circuits and I expect aliens. I expect Jennifer.

Instead, I find Kath.

"What are you *doing*?" I hiss.

"I woke up when you left the room, and I thought this was a good opportunity to practice my stealth," she explains. "I wanted to see if I could sneak up on you."

"Kath, you're the lookout. You don't even *need* to sneak."

"You don't know what the situation will call for."

"It calls for a lookout."

She *hmph*s and holds something out to me. "I grabbed these from my garage yesterday when I was packing my overnight bag. There's one for each of us."

"What is that?" I ask, looking at what appears to be a plastic brick with an antenna.

"You've never seen one?" She looks at me like I just admitted to having a tail. "It's a walkie-talkie, remember? An ancient relic from days past, for covert operations."

"Oh, right. I've just never seen one in real life." I take it from her, feeling my cheeks heat. "Isn't it easier to use our phones?"

Kath looks at me like, *You've never pulled a heist, and it shows.* "We're breaking the law, Mallory. We can't leave a *phone record.*"

"Oh." I stare at the walkie-talkie, feeling a bit ill. Maybe it's my lack of sleep. Or maybe that's just a normal way to feel when you're breaking into a missing girl's home to hunt for aliens.

"Let's start the Ms. Chan Watch. After she leaves, we can wake Ingrid." Kath plops onto my couch, sitting backward so her face is inches from the window. She looks comfortable, like she's decided she belongs, whether anyone else agrees or not. I don't know how she does it.

"What?" Kath gives me a look, and I realize that I'm just standing there, staring.

"Nothing," I say awkwardly, taking a seat beside her. There's a whole lot of space between us on the couch.

And, okay, the thing about a stakeout? There's a lot of silence. Five minutes pass, which feels like eternity. All I want to do is scream, even though that would be totally weird and also wake up my parents and ruin this whole operation. But I've never done well with silence. Part of me wishes Reagan were here. She always fills the room.

When I can't take it anymore, I blurt, "What happened to Ingrid?"

Kath raises her brows, and I realize that sounded rude.

"I mean," I clarify, "she seems different than she was a few years ago."

Kath shifts on the couch, and I recognize the discomfort on her face. How honest can you be without betraying your best friend? "I think it's mostly what happened with Pete."

Last year, Pete pulled some of his bullying stuff on Ingrid. It began in science class, when we started our botany unit and Ingrid was answering even more of our teacher's questions than usual. She always raised her hand super high and spoke so confidently, and she never, ever got anything wrong.

But about a week into the botany unit, Pete and his friends started, like, fake-coughing every time Ingrid raised her hand. I didn't know for sure, at first, but I got that sinking feeling. Something bad was happening.

Our science teacher realized something was happening a couple days after I did, but she couldn't prove anything, which meant she just stopped asking questions in class for a while.

So the coughing moved into the hallways, any time Pete and his friends passed Ingrid. And it became clearer what they were saying.

Shut her up. Cough. Cough. *Shut her up.*

It was mean. Pete's stuff always was. But it only lasted for a few days.

"I didn't think it was that bad," I say, "or it was, but it didn't last long."

Kath shoots me a look that says she doesn't quite buy what I'm saying. "Lots of things seem like they aren't that bad, as long as you don't look too closely."

"Right." But I *was* paying attention. Even Reagan said Pete went too far. And then when he stopped, it was a relief. It was over.

It just feels like there must be more to Ingrid, but Kath doesn't elaborate. We sink back into silence for a few very long moments. Kath chews her nail.

This time, she's the one who breaks. "Okay, I'm just gonna ask the question. Because I keep thinking it, and not saying it, and I hate that."

"Okay," I say. There's something serious in her tone that makes my heart drop.

"Do you feel guilty about Jennifer?"

I blink. My whole body reacts to her question: heart beating, palms sweating, as if a simple question is a full-on attack. As if words can physically hurt. I wonder how much Kath knows, and how she knows it, but I don't ask.

"Because *I* feel bad." She speaks quickly, like she wants to get the words out. "Look, don't tell Ingrid this, but I kind of . . . distanced us from Jennifer at school. You guys were mean to her on the first day, and then Pete started teasing her about capoeira, and after everything that happened with Ingrid, I didn't want to turn us into targets. It seemed easier to just . . . stay out of it."

I hesitate. "I get it." I guess that explains why Jennifer didn't hang out with them after that first week. I think about how Jennifer must have felt, with all those could-be friends turning their backs on her, and my throat hurts.

"I hate that I did that," Kath says, "and I hate that feeling. It's like I don't even know myself, because I want to think I'm a good person. I see people who don't do the right thing even though they *know* the right thing, and I always think . . . I want to be better than that."

My body flushes hot and cold at once, because it feels like she's talking about me, and what am I supposed to do with that?

But there's nothing confrontational in her tone, and she seems lost in her own world, so I say, "Maybe it's more complicated than knowing the right thing. Maybe people are just trying to balance helping other people and keeping themselves safe."

"Maybe." She frowns. "But sometimes I think *complicated*

123

is the word people use when they don't want to think too hard."

Again, it's kind of a jab at me, and I start to feel frustrated, because I don't want to sit here while she tells me I'm a bad person. But there's the tiniest whisper that maybe she's right.

I sigh. "I do feel bad."

Kath looks surprised by that, and I wonder if she really thinks I'm such a bad person that I wouldn't care. She doesn't even know about the Incident. She thinks I'm only talking about what happened in the cafeteria.

"So why do you hang out with Tess and Reagan?" she asks. "They're awful."

I should defend my friends. That's what a good person would do. I should tell Kath that she doesn't know what she's talking about. But what comes out is: "I don't hang out with them."

My betrayal of Reagan pools in my stomach and I squeeze my eyes shut. I can't do anything right. If I try to befriend one person, I end up betraying another.

Kath snorts. "Up until two days ago you did."

"I know Reagan can get intense," I say, choosing my words carefully, channeling Dad. "But she has a lot going on in her life. More than most people realize."

Kath shakes her head. "A lot of people have stuff going on, and they aren't rude to everyone."

"Reagan's not rude to everyone. She can be really nice, to me."

I sound so needy that I want to take my words back, but instead I keep going, filling silence. "And as for Tess, Reagan wanted to be friends with her, so it just kind of happened. Sometimes I like her, but sometimes . . ."

Kath says simply, "Tess is the worst."

"She is! She's the worst!"

That startles a laugh out of Kath, and I smile back in surprise. Here we are: *bonding*. And thanks to Tess, of all people.

"She gave me hair advice once." Kath rolls her eyes. "Which I did not ask for. She told me she could fix my frizz. You know, because she has curly hair, too, and she thinks that's the same thing."

"That sounds like Tess. Sometimes you just want to shake her and say, *This isn't about you!*"

"Exactly. And the way she talks," Kath says, "like everything is a question? It's awful? I sit next to her in math, and whenever Mr. Moore calls on her, she always acts like she doesn't know. Even though I can see the answer right there on her paper! She does know!"

Now I'm laughing, mostly with relief. This conversation is so much easier—I can breathe again. "Oh, trust me. She does that with everything. Reagan and I always joke about it."

"If you know an answer, *own it*. Be smart. Not knowing stuff doesn't make you cool."

"Yeah, we can't stand her," I agree.

And then we both stop. The smiles slide off our faces. It's so easy to talk bad about someone. It's so easy to bond

125

over hating someone else. It's almost scary how naturally it comes.

"I'm sure she has some good qualities, deep down," Kath backtracks. "And the question-talking thing isn't hurting anybody."

"Yeah, I know. I didn't mean it." But I did mean it. That's the worst part. How have I spent so long being friends with someone I don't like? It's turned *me* into someone I don't like.

Kath looks away. "I'm not, like . . . mean."

I almost don't hear her. She doesn't sound like herself—not confident and blunt as usual.

"I don't think you are," I say.

Her expression says she doesn't believe that. "I actually try, you know. I try not to be emotional, because people freak out when I am. But then they think I'm cold and mean. I can't win.

"And I don't say anything about the hymns we have to sing in chapel. I play *Christmas carols* in the orchestra, all year round. But then I miss a few days of school in the fall for the Jewish holidays, and all of a sudden it's a *thing*."

She kind of laughs, in a not-funny way. "I heard Kyle say that I'm off-putting. That's what people think. And sometimes I don't know if it's because I'm Black or because I'm Jewish or because I'm me. Maybe a mix of all three."

I realize with twisting dread that maybe I kind of thought that about her, too. "I'm sorry," I say.

When she doesn't respond, I add, "My mom talks about stuff like that, like all the racism that happens to Asian

126

people. Like I know it was wrong that Pete made fun of Jennifer for doing 'kung fu.' " I realize after I say it that I've made air quotes with one finger instead of two. The reminder of Mom makes me kind of sad. I wish I could talk to her about this stuff without it being a thing.

"Oh, yeah. That racist stuff definitely happened with Jennifer," Kath says. "Does it happen with you, too?"

I hesitate. "I don't think so." The truth is, I've never really thought about it. And maybe that's because of my no-intellectual-curiosity problem.

But there are little things sometimes, like when Tess said Jennifer and I were similar, and I didn't know if it was because we were both Asian or because there's something Jennifer-ish deep inside me. I don't know which answer makes me feel more uncomfortable, and maybe that's the prickly part of it. There are all these little maybe-things, where I don't know whether something's racist but it worms into my head anyway.

"I don't know," I correct.

There's a flicker of recognition on Kath's face. "People can be the worst."

I nod, wondering if that's true. Wondering, too, how often "people" includes me.

The morning light begins to trickle through my living room windows. Birds start chirping. It's nearly 5 a.m.

"Hey, Kath?" There's a question I want to ask, and I'm worried that once it's truly light out, I won't be able to.

"Yeah?" She looks a little nervous, too, as if she knows

the rising sun might change things between us, and she's not quite ready for that.

"Do you really think people can become better? Like, through human evolution or even just, like, growing up?"

She stares out the window, at Jennifer's closed front door. Her voice is quiet. "Sometimes."

Kath sounds so sad that it hurts my heart a little, but then she turns to me and adds, "I guess I do. Probably for the same reason Jennifer believes in aliens."

I frown. "Because you saw some crop circles?"

"No." She snorts, then grows serious. "Because it's too lonely not to."

I shift on the couch. This conversation has gotten way too deep for comfort. "Wow."

She laughs.

And thankfully, finally, Jennifer's front door opens. We snap our focus back to our mission as Ms. Chan steps out of the house. She walks to her car in the driveway. When she clicks her keys, the headlights flash once, twice.

She opens the door, about to get in, and then stops, staring off into the distance at nothing in particular, letting a few long moments slip past.

Then she takes a breath and gets into her car, pulls out of her driveway, down the street.

"Let's wake Ingrid," I whisper.

It's go time.

17

I stand in front of Jennifer Chan's front door. Entering feels wrong. But we're doing it for the right reasons, I keep reminding myself.

Static explodes out of my walkie-talkie, followed by Kath's voice: "Go inside."

I turn to see her on my couch, watching through the window. Ingrid peeks out from the side of the Chan house, where she's waiting under Jennifer's room, and gives me a thumbs-up.

I place my hand on the doorknob, and then I'm remembering meeting Jennifer for the first time and hearing her ask, *Can I trust you?*

I squeeze my eyes shut.

What if I'm walking into something bigger than I can possibly understand?

I turn the knob and step inside.

The house is quiet and empty, and I'm hit with this overwhelming sense of longing, like the house itself is missing

Jennifer. But I push through the feeling and walk past glass baking trays full of neighbors' home-cooked meals, past a family of half-full, lipstick-stained ceramic mugs on the counter, past the stale scent of incense and old food that hangs in the air.

I make my legs climb the steps up to Jennifer's room.

The floorboards creak as I enter, and once I'm inside, I can see she's unpacked a lot more since summer. Her desk is lined with glitter pens, shiny library books, and cratered rocks that look like tiny asteroids. Her purple-painted walls are adorned with two posters of astronauts smiling in their NASA suits—Mae Jemison and Leroy Chiao, according to their labels. Jennifer stuck them to the wall with duct tape, the cute kind with cartoon ducks on it.

Her green apple sheets are crumpled, like she's just stepped out of bed and will be back any moment. Seeing all this, I feel rooted to the floor. This room is so wonderfully, horribly *Jennifer*.

Kath's voice crackles over the walkie-talkie. "Did you find it? Over."

I jump and turn the volume knob as low as it can go. "Kath, chill. I just got inside."

"Hurry up. Over."

Now Ingrid's voice bursts from my walkie-talkie. "I agree with Kath. Please hurry. I'm standing out in the open like a criminal. Over."

My voice cracks when I speak, and I hope they think it's just static. "Ms. Chan will be out looking for Jennifer all day. But I'm still trying to hurry."

And with that, I get moving, rummaging through her bookshelves.

The walkie-talkie crackles. "You have to say 'over,'" Kath says.

"Kath, seriously," I respond. "I'm going to turn this thing off if you keep distracting me."

"Don't you dare do that. You're cutting me out of the fun, and besides, you need me. Over."

Ignoring her, I open all the dresser drawers. Nothing but clothes.

The walkie flares up again. "Also, you still didn't say 'over.' Over."

I whip it out of my pocket and turn it off. Then I check the desk drawers. Nothing.

I check the remaining boxes. Nothing there, either, aside from winter coats that are far too heavy for Florida.

I step back and survey the room, playing the whole *if I were a stack of alien-hunting journals, where would I hide* game. I come up with nothing.

And then a terrible thought occurs to me: *What if Jennifer took the journals with her?* It makes sense. She might need them in her alien hunt. And if that's the case—then we've reached another dead end.

Hands shaking, I search the dresser drawers again. Just in case. Just hoping.

I'm on my knees, digging through her pants drawer, when I find something soft and neon orange crumpled in the back—a familiar T-shirt with the words ALIENS WALK AMONG US!

That shirt.

My heart catches as I run my thumb over the worn cotton. I didn't even think she heard me when I told her not to wear it. But now I picture her stuffing it into the back of the drawer, and something cold burns in my chest. I thought I was helping.

I'm still staring at that shirt when I hear a creak behind me. I scream, jump up, spin around.

"Quiet! Quiet!" Kath shouts. She runs over and clamps a sweaty hand over my mouth. "You are the worst spy of all time!"

I tug her hand off. "What are you doing here? You were supposed to keep watch!"

She shrugs. "You said Ms. Chan's gone all day. Plus, you muted me and I didn't like that."

I shake my head. "Kath. You're endangering this whole heist."

She starts opening the desk drawers. "Am I? Because you haven't found the journals, and you clearly need my help."

"Fine," I concede, folding the shirt in my hands.

She pauses, noticing what I'm holding for the first time. Then she looks back at my face, searching for something, though I'm not sure what. "Are you okay?" she asks.

I stuff the shirt back into the drawer and clear my throat. *Focus.* "I was just worried that maybe Jennifer took the journals with her."

Kath thinks for a moment. "Nah."

"What if she brought them with her for reference or something?"

"They would have weighed her down. She wrote them. She knows what's in them."

I'm starting to get frustrated. Kath can't know these things for sure. "I guess, but—"

She taps a finger to her lips. "If you had highly sensitive information, where would you hide it?"

"I checked her drawers, but—"

Without warning, she drops to her hands and knees and pats the floorboards. She shuffles across the floor, digging her nails into each seam.

"Seriously?" I say. "Under the floorboards?"

Kath looks up. "Are you gonna criticize or are you gonna help?"

Sighing, I kneel beside her and pat the floor like I'm trying to reassure it. I'm feeling real silly, until suddenly one of the floorboards slides against my fingertips, lifting to reveal a hidden cubby.

"Oh my god," I breathe. "Kath. You were *right*."

There, in that small, cobwebbed space, is a stack of composition notebooks.

"I told you!" Kath says, scrambling over to me. "This is so cool!"

"I guess you and Jennifer think alike." I grab a handful of Jennifer's notebooks, and Kath takes the rest before sliding the floorboard back into place with her foot. We run to the window, then drop them down one by one to Ingrid, who catches them and hides them in the bushes. But just after I drop the last journal, Ingrid swears and ducks into the shrubbery, hiding with all those notebooks.

"What are you *doing*?" Kath hisses.

Then we hear it. The slam of a car door in the driveway, followed by the open and close of the front door.

Kath and I freeze.

"I thought you said Ms. Chan leaves all day," Kath whispers, just as I say, "This is why we needed a lookout."

Footsteps start up the stairs, and Kath moves toward the door, but I pull her back. "We can't go out that way. We'll run right into her."

We turn to the window. But we're on the second floor.

"We could climb down," Kath whispers.

"Um . . ." I stare down at the bushes beneath Jennifer's window. And then at the very flimsy drainpipe. "No thank you."

"You'd rather get caught?"

Kath doesn't wait for my response. She hoists herself over the windowsill and grabs the drainpipe. "Come on!" she whisper-shouts.

The footsteps get closer. I only have a few seconds. Kath scoots down the pipe, and I look at the ground. My vision goes in and out. If I climb down, I'll faint or fall or both. But if I stay, I'll get caught.

I grab on to the windowsill, ready to swing my legs over, but my whole body seizes up. There's no way I'm doing this.

Kath's halfway down now, and the footsteps are right outside the door.

As the knob begins to turn, I cross the distance between the window and Jennifer's bed and roll under it, sliding beneath the mattress just as the door swings open.

For a moment, everything's still. The only sound is my

heart, roaring in my ears. It's so loud that I know Jennifer's mom hears me.

The floorboards creak as she walks across the room. She pauses, standing next to the dresser, and my nerves go wild. *She knows, she knows, she knows.*

Sure enough, I watch her stockinged feet as she walks over to the window. She pauses again—and then I realize.

The window. That window was closed and we opened it.

I can't see anything above her ankles, but in my imagination, I watch her leaning out the window, looking at the bent drainpipe, then farther down. I hope hard, with everything that I have, that Kath made it down already, that she and Ingrid ran back to my house, that the notebooks are hidden well enough in the bushes.

I count my heartbeats—*one two threefourfive*—

Rebecca Chan clears her throat. *She knows.* Her voice is a croak.

"Jennifer?" she calls out.

It's enough to stop my heartbeats all together.

She doesn't know.

Because of course she sees the open window and thinks it's Jennifer. Of course. And this—this is so much worse than being caught. Without meaning to, I've given her hope, and the hope is a lie.

What can I do? I can't roll out now.

She walks over, and the mattress sags under her as she sits. I stare up at the box springs, just above my nose.

I hold my breath, waiting with this unbearable feeling of dread.

She inhales. Exhales. Presses her toes against the wood.

Beneath her feet is a secret board, with a secret space—empty now.

I listen to her breath, slow and ragged.

Please don't cry. Please don't cry. I'm silently begging Rebecca Chan, but suddenly I'm pleading with myself, too.

Suddenly I have all these tears inside me, sitting right on my chest. I picture my heart-springs, sagging under their weight.

I don't even know where these tears came from, but my chest spasms with the need to sob. I bite my cheek to keep the sadness in. How did I get here—how did this seem like a good idea a few hours ago? It feels like forever that I'm lying there, and the whole time, *she doesn't know.*

She doesn't know I'm here. She doesn't know I'm trying to find her daughter. She doesn't know that we just took all of Jennifer's journals. She doesn't know that Jennifer gave me one, to read and borrow and understand.

She doesn't know about the Incident.

We stood there in that bathroom just days before Jennifer ran—Reagan and Tess and me surrounding her, pressing her against the wall, nowhere for her to go.

My chest shudders and I hold every muscle still, afraid to even breathe, because it's all threatening to spill out.

Then

18

The end of everything started with a buzz.

A couple days after the kung fu face-off, I was sitting with Tess at our lunch table, waiting for Reagan because the math honors class always ran late.

Tess was telling me about some personality quiz she found online, some kind of number or category or type that perfectly fit her, and she was trying to convince me to take it. To be honest, I hated those personality tests. I always felt like I was getting the questions wrong, which freaked me out, because they're supposed to be easy. I'm supposed to know myself.

But I was nodding along, pretending to consider it, and that's when we heard it. The double *buzz-buzz* of our group chat, both our phones going off at once.

Tess grabbed hers first, whipping it out of her pocket before I could even react. She laughed loudly, clapping her hand over her mouth.

I fumbled for mine, and when I finally pulled the chat open, I felt something shift inside me, a tiny rip.

Reagan had sent a picture of Jennifer in math class, sitting a few desks away. Her sweatshirt billowed unflatteringly around her stomach. She was rubbing her eye. Her hair was a mess.

Reagan's message followed: WHAT A WRECK.

Tess shook her head. "Honestly, we know she's a lost cause, but she should at least *try* to look good? Like, make an *effort*?"

I felt bad looking, but it took me a few seconds to pull my eyes from the screen. Feelings tumbled in my stomach—fear and guilt and something unnameable, too. Tess didn't notice my silence, and I slipped my phone into my pocket, hoping to never mention it again.

But when Reagan arrived a few minutes later, sliding her lunch tray beside mine, she nudged me and said, "Why didn't you respond?"

Her tone was light, and I knew she expected me to join in the fun. Part of me wanted to. I felt myself tilt in her direction, but I tried to resist.

"Sorry, I didn't see your message," I lied.

Tess leaned forward. "Um, yeah you did? We literally just looked at it, like, two minutes ago?"

Reagan stared at me, and I realized that without meaning to, I'd taken a side. In just one slice of a second, I'd chosen Jennifer over Reagan, and Reagan wouldn't forgive that. Because best friends were supposed to support each other. They weren't supposed to judge or make each other feel like bad people.

"Sorry," I said, not quite meeting Reagan's eyes. "It was funny."

"What's funny is that Jennifer, like, worships herself?" Tess said. "Like she's so cocky, which is hilarious, because she has no reason to be."

I hesitated. "I don't know if she's cocky."

I expected annoyance from Reagan, but instead, I got sympathy. "Mal, don't be naive. Did you see the way she looked at us that first day? The way she looked at *you*? She felt bad for you, because she thinks she's better."

I chewed my cheek. That felt kind of true. And ever since that day with Pete, part of me had wondered: *Was* she better?

I didn't ask the question, but Reagan read it on my face. "Mal, nobody has the right to make you feel that way. We love you just the way you are, and you don't have to change."

Gratitude stung my eyes, but I blinked back the tears. This was what best friends were for.

"Jennifer just exists on a different planet," I said finally. I didn't know if it was a compliment or an insult. "She needs someone to bring her down to Earth."

Reagan laughed. "That's exactly it."

I thought that was the end of it, but the next day, Tess sent another photo to our group chat. One from PE—Jennifer sweaty, hair sticking to her cheeks.

And suddenly this sort-of-joke became a force, as unstoppable as gravity.

Over the next few weeks, whenever we saw Jennifer, my

friends would sneak their phones out, trying to catch her at her worst, trying to capture the ugliest photo possible.

It was mostly Reagan and Tess sending pictures.

But also, just a little, me.

The first time I snapped a photo—Jennifer running down the hallway, late for class, totally unaware that her backpack and posture made her look like a sprinting turtle—those stomach-churning feelings grew stronger.

And suddenly I recognized that unnameable feeling.

Relief.

Because for a little while, I wasn't worrying about myself. Thinking about how other people saw me was like this impossible, constant weight. And now, for a few moments, I was free.

Of all the tricks Reagan had taught me, this one was the best.

I knew it was wrong. But it was addictive. And I didn't think Jennifer would ever know. It was just in our private chat. We weren't saving or screenshotting the photos, so I figured, if it wasn't hurting anyone, then maybe, surely, I wasn't doing any harm.

Now

19

It could have been worse.

Jennifer's mom left the house again without realizing I was under the bed, and I sprinted back home just before my parents woke up. Overall, Kath, Ingrid, and I were successful. We got what we needed.

But I'm shaken.

This is real. Jennifer's mom is hurting—and Jennifer might be, too.

Now it's finally lunch period and I'm walking through the school hallways toward the chapel, my backpack heavy with the weight of Jennifer's journals, when I run straight into Reagan.

"Uh, hey?" she says with a half laugh.

"Oh, hi. Um, I actually have to run." I try to step past her, but she blocks my path.

"Aren't you going to lunch?"

I've never skipped lunch period with Tess and Reagan. It's usually my favorite part of the day.

"Actually, ah, I'm just heading to the library," I lie. "I have to finish something up . . . for science."

She frowns. We're not in the same science section, but our assignments are always the same. "What? The worksheet? You can copy mine during lunch."

"No," I say, dragging the word as I wait for another lie to pop into my head. Around us, hand-painted poster boards proclaim WE LOVE YOU, JENNIFER and JENNIFER, COME HOME!

Reagan follows my gaze and rolls her eyes. "Yeah, everyone's making those signs. People act like they care, but I think they just feel bad."

I can't tell if her comment is directed at me or if it's casual, a thought tossed aside.

I shift my backpack uncomfortably, and Reagan glances at it. There's no possible way she knows what's in my bag, but somehow it feels like she can sense Jennifer's notebooks.

"You're acting so weird," she says, her tone half concern, half accusation.

"I'm sorry," I respond. And I am. All I want to do is eat lunch with her and Tess, pretend this never happened, and just feel okay. Maybe I could, if I let myself.

But that wouldn't be the right thing to do—not with Jennifer still out there. Something in my chest twists, and I wonder if I'll always have to choose between doing good and feeling good.

"I . . . have to go," I say.

When I turn to leave, she calls out, "Mal. Wait."

A few kids glance over as they pass in the hallway, and Reagan plasters on a fake smile. *Everything's fine,* it tells the world. But to me, it says, *I'm not okay.*

She steps forward and lowers her voice. Her smile falters. "I need you. And I feel like I'm losing you."

I want to stay with her and make her worries disappear, like a best friend should. But I can't think of anything to say. I can't think of anything except Jennifer.

"You're not losing me," I tell her. I don't know if that's another lie.

This time, I leave before she has the chance to respond.

The chapel's media tech room is cramped. On one side, there's a long table for all the sound and light control panels, as well as the school radio system. On the other is an empty desk surrounded by four chairs. When I get there, Kath and Ingrid are already crammed around the panels, and there's hardly room for me.

The only thing that keeps it from feeling claustrophobic is the large window that looks out at the chapel—but right now I wish it weren't there. Even though the chapel is always open, being here feels wrong. There's something eerie about being in this space with no one to fill it.

I turn my back to the window.

"Did you search for clues?" I ask. "Can you tell if anyone scheduled the assembly signal?"

Kath chews her fingernail. "I looked for signs of tampering, but I can't find anything. It doesn't look like anyone was in here at all."

I take a breath. "Which makes aliens seem even more likely."

Ingrid frowns, like she doesn't want to believe but is maybe, just a little, starting to. "If that's the case," she says, "then we better get to work."

I pull the journals out of my backpack and scatter them across the empty desk. Then we each grab a chair, pick a journal, and get to work.

"This is . . . a lot," Kath says, paging through Volume V.

As I flip through Jennifer's research and theories, I try to avoid the sections where Jennifer wrote about her own life. Reading it makes me feel . . . squicky. Guilty. Her journals are so personal, and these thoughts weren't meant for me.

"This *is* a lot," Ingrid agrees. "But none of it's recent. These entries are from last year, at the latest. Did you find anything more recent in her room?"

I think about the notebook Jennifer let me borrow—the most recent volume, hidden under my bed. "No," I say, too quickly. "But I'm sure we can find what we need in these."

Kath frowns. "But wouldn't she have written *more* if she had a breakthrough that made her leave? Don't we need to know why, exactly, she ran?"

"Let's worry about the *where*, not the *why*," I insist.

Kath looks like she's about to disagree, but Ingrid interrupts.

"Look at this: Jennifer transcribed a quote from a woman

144

who says she was abducted by aliens. 'It was like an out-of-body experience. I couldn't escape, not even if I wanted to, and I didn't want to. My body floated in a bright wash of light, and I could see the whole world, my whole life, and I wasn't alone.' " Ingrid tilts her head. "That doesn't sound much like an abduction."

Kath points to another entry. "Well, how about this one? This guy says he was sucked into the sky by a bolt of lightning."

Ingrid wrinkles her nose, but I'm too busy reading through a different volume to comment. Jennifer recorded UFO sighting and alien abduction stories, and she had a whole lot of ideas about why certain people saw them.

Maybe some people just understand the world better than others, she wrote. *Or maybe there's something some people need to understand, and the aliens are trying to tell them.*

My discomfort grows stronger, and I skip past those pages until I find some entries about Area 51.

"She thinks aliens are here to shut down the weapons facilities," I say, nudging the notebook toward Kath and Ingrid.

Kath skims it before reading aloud, " 'Almost all UFO sightings are concentrated around military areas—and often ones with nuclear testing facilities.' "

Ingrid hesitates. "Well, if the sightings are usually near these facilities, we have to consider the possibility that people are seeing secret military weapons, which they're mistaking for aliens."

"Maybe they're seeing secret military weapons. But that doesn't explain the other signs," I say.

We all look at each other.

"What if this is real?" I whisper.

Kath takes a deep breath. Ingrid taps her fingers.

"I don't know," Kath says.

I hate that that's the best answer any of us can give, and I turn back to Jennifer's notes. The answer is in here. It has to be.

I flip through pages, faster and faster, though I barely know what I'm looking for.

And then, at the end of Volume VI, I find the heading: *The Right Number.*

"Oh my god," I murmur.

Kath and Ingrid lean over my shoulder, and breathlessly, heart pounding, I point to Jennifer's words. "'I did it,'" I read. "'I finally figured it out.'"

Jennifer Chan's Guide to the Universe
Volume VI, Entry No. 51: The Right Number

I did it! I finally figured it out!

1420 megahertz. It's the frequency made by hydrogen atoms, which were all created in the big bang. Which means hydrogen has been everywhere, since forever. No matter how different they are from us, aliens and humans will have hydrogen in common.

And we'll have this frequency in common, too.

1420 megahertz.

That's the frequency SETI, the organization searching for extraterrestrial intelligence, uses when they send their signals. So that's what I'll do. I'll use the same number as the scientists. Of course!

And I'll be successful, because I'm not afraid to believe.

Famous scientist Carl Sagan once said there were more stars in the universe than all the grains of sand on Earth. I mean, that's a lot of stars! The chances of intelligent life out there are astronomical.

So then here's my question: Why are people so afraid to believe?

Now

20

"1420 megahertz," Ingrid repeats, reading Jennifer's journal entry. Turning to Kath, she asks, "Can you tune the school radio to that frequency?"

Kath bites a nail. "I can try, but this radio is only meant to operate at 460 megahertz. If I tune it higher, it won't broadcast on the school intercom, but I'm not *positive* it'll reach into space."

Kath's uncertainty doesn't stop us from hoping. We rush to the radio control panel and watch as Kath punches in codes and turns dials.

"Okay," she says finally. "It's tuned. What do we want to say?"

I pause. All this time trying to find the right number, and we never considered the right *message*.

"It's unlikely they'd understand English," Ingrid says.

"That's true," I admit. "But maybe we could still try . . . 'hi'?"

Kath shrugs. "Simple enough." Then she leans forward into the microphone and says, in the most dramatic radio voice she can muster, *"Hi."*

We hold our breaths. Seconds tick away.

"Now what?" I whisper.

"We wait," Ingrid says.

And so we do. We stare at the machine for five whole minutes, getting more and more fidgety by the second.

"We should expect a delay," Ingrid says. Her voice sounds so loud after the long silence that I kind of jump. "It takes a while for a signal to travel into space. And then if they respond, the signal would have to travel back down, which would take even *more* time."

"Right," I say. A few more minutes go by.

"Or this radio isn't strong enough," Kath repeats, like if she explains it well enough, this will all feel okay. "Its broadcast signal is only meant to reach across the school grounds, so reaching into space is a big ask."

Ingrid nods along, but I can't help but feel like this is my fault. Like I didn't try hard enough, or *care* hard enough.

"Jennifer said that if you want aliens to listen, you have to show them you believe," I say. "She said you have to shout it to the whole world, so everyone can hear you."

Kath blinks. "Is that supposed to be a metaphor?"

"I'm pretty sure she meant it literally. When I slept over, she literally shouted to the sky that she believed."

"And that's what you want to do?" Ingrid asks.

I hesitate. "I know it sounds weird, but Jennifer's been right so far."

Kath tilts her head. "So, what, you're gonna walk into the cafeteria and shout, *'Listen up, everybody! I'm a believer!'*"

"Well, maybe."

Kath and Ingrid exchange a glance.

"What?" I ask.

Ingrid frowns. "You're not very . . . you know."

"I don't know."

After a long pause, Ingrid says, "You don't like to shake things up. You kind of . . . follow what everyone else does."

"That's not true." Spots flash in front of my eyes, and I lean forward to rest my hand on the table. The Incident pushes its way out from the back of my mind. Reagan's words ring in my ears. *Who do you think you are?*

"I'm not like that," I say.

Ingrid and Kath exchange another glance, speaking in that silent best-friend language, and it's like I'm outside my own body, seeing myself through their eyes.

But they don't know me. They don't know who I am.

I drag a chair into the center of the media tech room. When I stand up on it, it wobbles beneath my feet and I throw my hands out by my sides, suddenly afraid I'll fall.

Kath's eyebrows shoot up. "What's happening?"

"I'm shaking things up," I respond. "I believe."

"Yes, Mal," Ingrid says carefully. "We know."

It's not the middle of the cafeteria. I'm not announcing it to the whole grade. It's just Kath and Ingrid, and the chapel's media tech room is soundproof. But still. This makes me feel self-conscious.

"I'm proving a point," I say.

"You don't have to," Ingrid says. "It's fine."

It's not fine, though. I don't want to be the person they think I am.

Spreading my arms wider, I repeat, "I believe." Then even louder, "I believe in aliens!"

Right now, in this chapel, it's like I'm daring myself to believe in something. And in return, daring aliens or God or *something* to exist.

In this sliver-slice of time, everything in the galaxy is connected and I feel big, like I could fill the universe, and I'm not scared of it.

My heart thunders. I'm half expecting another *Wow!* signal. But outside of myself, the chapel is still empty, still silent. Still.

"Please." The word slips out. I'm begging for something. But nothing.

Suddenly I feel very, very silly.

I think about Jennifer's journal entry: *Why are people so afraid to believe?* Well, Jennifer, maybe because it's impossibly embarrassing to be proven wrong.

Shaky and way too aware of Kath's and Ingrid's eyes on me, I start to climb down.

"Wait!" Kath says. She looks startled at first, like she didn't expect to say anything. Then she grabs her chair, drags it in front of mine, and stands up beside me. "I believe in aliens, too!"

"What are you doing?" I ask. I kind of think she's making fun of me, but she shrugs.

"I'm showing solidarity. And, you know, if this is what we need to do to make contact, well . . ." She throws a pointed look at Ingrid.

Ingrid blows out a breath, halfway between a laugh and

a sigh. "Fine. Fine." Then she, too, drags over a chair, stands on it, and announces, "I don't necessarily *believe,* but I am willing to entertain the poss—"

"Ingrid!" Kath scolds.

Ingrid throws her hands up. "I figured the aliens would appreciate *honesty.*"

"And how do you think that makes them feel?"

Ingrid nods as if this is a reasonable argument and corrects, "Okay, fine, regarding our current situation, I have decided to believe in alien contact. Maybe temporarily. But. I do believe."

While I watch them, the ridiculousness of the three of us, standing on these chairs in the middle of a cramped room, shouting at aliens, strikes me. All at once, I'm laughing and I can't stop.

"What?" Kath asks, though she cracks a smile, too.

"I didn't expect that," I admit.

And then they're both grinning, and I throw my arms out wider and shout, "I BELIEVE IN ALIENS."

"I ALSO BELIEVE IN ALIENS," Kath shouts, even louder than me.

And Ingrid chimes in, "TEMPORARILY, ME TOO."

I turn to them and add, "AND WE'RE GOING TO FIND THEM."

I'm grinning, feeling weird, but happy-weird. Like this is the most embarrassing, cringey thing I've ever done, but I don't care. It feels good, giddy, and I'm doing it with my friends.

Maybe I am not the scared, nervous girl I thought I was.

Maybe I am someone new, someone fearless. And maybe I don't need anyone else to see that in me. Maybe it's enough to see it in myself. I feel suspended, almost, like I'm floating above all my guilt and worry, and I'm just me.

And then Ingrid's eyes flick behind me, and that smile drops right off her face. Kath's gaze lands on the same spot, and she scrambles off the chair.

Slowly, very slowly, I turn to see Tess, standing alone in the chapel. She's staring at us through the window, her face dancing with an unsettling mixture of disgust and delight.

Instantly, my cheeks go fire-hot and I start to sweat. I want to jump down and hide under this chair.

Leave, I silently beg Tess. *Please leave.*

I wish I could will away this embarrassment. I felt so free, shouting to the world, daring it to see me. Now I don't know how to find my way back there, and I finally recognize the way I felt when I first watched Jennifer shout into the sky.

I was jealous. I was jealous that she could live in that freedom, because I didn't know if I could ever hold on to that feeling—and I still don't.

Tess walks up to the media tech room and knocks on the door. Kath, Ingrid, and I turn to each other in silent panic before eventually deciding that there's no use ignoring her.

Kath lets her in.

"Um?" Tess asks as soon as she's through the doorway.

At least she's efficient. No need to ask, *Who are you and what did you do with Mallory?* when a single syllable works just fine.

Kath narrows her eyes, but I respond before she can say anything.

"Tess, hey," I say, as close to normal as possible. "What are you doing here?"

"Praying?" she says, like, *duh*. "I had a few minutes before next period, so I came here to pray for Jennifer?"

Hearing that Tess is praying for Jennifer surprises me. Maybe she cares more than I realized.

"That's . . . good." My limbs finally seem to work, and I climb off the chair. "But, um, we should probably get to class."

"So, you believe in aliens?" Tess scrunches her nose like she can smell the *weird* on me. "I guess that's not surprising. You've always believed the wrong things."

Dread stirs in my chest. I thought this room was sound-proof, but maybe that doesn't apply when you're shouting at the top of your lungs.

"Shouting about aliens was a joke," I say automatically, and then I regret it. I reach for that feeling of freedom, but it's slippery. It escapes my grasp.

"A joke," Tess repeats. "Totally."

By the end of the day, everyone's gonna know about this. I might as well have broadcast it to the whole school.

All I want is for Tess to leave, but instead, she takes a step closer and I realize, too late, what's lying on the desk.

I make a move to push the journals away, but she's already seen the writing on the covers: *JENNIFER CHAN'S GUIDE TO THE UNIVERSE*.

For a second, her eyes widen, and there's no hiding the fear. Then they narrow. "What are you doing, Mal?"

"None of your business," Kath says, and I jump a little. I almost forgot Kath and Ingrid were there.

"Um, actually, Kath, it kind of is my business?" Tess says. "So you might want to back off."

Ingrid winces, but Kath just sighs, immune to the threat in Tess's voice.

"Leave her alone," I tell Tess.

She looks between the three of us, and I watch her put the pieces together. "Are you three looking for Jennifer?"

"Uh . . . yes," I admit, because I don't know how to hide it. "I care about this, Tess. Don't you?"

I scan her face for any sign of guilt or concern, but I can't read her.

I'm starting to wonder how well I really know Tess—and how much I just decided I know her because it made things easier. She was always someone I could hide behind.

Tess rolls her eyes. "Obviously I care. That's why I'm praying?"

"But what if we could do more than pray? What if we could—?"

"I just don't think you should get involved?" Tess folds her arms over her chest and glances at the journals.

I want to tell her that I already *was* involved—and she

was, too—but I don't want Kath and Ingrid to ask any questions. I don't want them to know what we did.

Tess and I lock eyes.

I won't tell anyone about the Incident, I tell her. I can say a lot without saying a word.

Tess takes a deep breath, and the tension in her shoulders releases a little. "I don't know what happened to you," she says. "But if you want to be part of some creepy Jennifer fan club, then fine."

"Okay," I say. The adrenaline racing through my body has transformed into a pounding headache.

She turns like she's about to leave, and then says, all fake-casual, "And if you want to find out more about Jennifer, why don't you ask Pete?"

"I doubt Pete knows more than us," Ingrid mumbles.

"Oh yeah?" Tess can't stop her gossip-grin. "Because I heard from Erika, who heard from Kyle, that Pete had a huge crush on her."

Thinking of Reagan, I blurt, "He had a crush? On Jennifer? That can't be true."

Ingrid lets out the smallest scoff, and Tess shrugs. "But you didn't hear it from me."

I'm tempted to ask if Reagan knows, but I don't want to give Tess the satisfaction.

"Plus," Tess continues, "Erika saw him talking to Jennifer after school, the same day as the orchestra concert."

I blink. "And you didn't think to tell me that?"

"Um, you've been a little busy?" Tess gestures to Kath and Ingrid, looking almost hurt.

Kath steps forward. "You mean this happened right before Jennifer ran away?"

Tess shrugs. "That's what Erika said."

Ingrid, Kath, and I stare at each other.

"Well, if that's true," I say slowly, "then Pete was the last person to see Jennifer Chan."

21

We have a ten-minute break to change classes before last period, and that's when Kath, Ingrid, and I decide to talk to Pete.

And by *talk,* I mean Kath kinda corners him by the lockers and drags him into the stairwell.

Ingrid's uncomfortable with all this, I can tell, and after Pete's bullying, I don't blame her.

But now Ingrid, Kath, and I are trapped in a stairwell with him. Or maybe he's trapped in a stairwell with us, because as soon as the door slams shut, Kath pelts him with questions. "What did you do to Jennifer the day she went missing? Were you mean to her? Did you say something that made her run away?"

It's a horrible thing, but I almost wish Pete *did* say something to hurt Jennifer. Because at least then I wouldn't be the only one.

"Calm down." Pete raises a hand, like he's trying to hold us back. "You don't need to interrogate me. I was just asking Jennifer something."

"And we need you to tell us what that was," I explain, trying to sound *calm*, though that's pretty difficult, considering the circumstances.

"Uh." He stares at us, totally freaked out and a little lost, like he's starring in a TV show and we're side characters who have suddenly gone off script. "Why?"

I swallow. This is about us getting information from Pete. Not the other way around.

But before I can tell him that, Ingrid confesses, "We're looking for her."

Kath and I turn to give Ingrid *What the heck?* eyes, but she just looks down at her hands. "What? Tess knows. He'd find out soon enough."

Pete's whole expression goes from guarded to surprised. "What do you mean, you're looking for her?"

"It's self-explanatory," Kath says.

Pete frowns. "You know my dad and the police are doing a whole search, right?"

"I don't trust the police," Kath says.

Pete bristles. "They sent out an Amber Alert and they're interviewing her mom and teachers. And they posted on Facebook or whatever. They're doing their jobs."

"But did they interview you—the last person to talk to Jennifer?"

"Well, no, because I'm not involved," he says, as if this is oh-so-obvious. "And it's not important."

Kath's jaw tightens. "You don't get to decide what's important right now. Do you realize how wrong it is to hold any information back?"

I blink. Pete's focused on Kath. Kath's focused on Pete. Ingrid's focused on her hands. Nobody's looking at me—which is good, because Kath's words make me dizzy.

What would she say if she knew what I'm holding back?

"What we talked about . . . it doesn't have anything to do with her running away," Pete says. Then he shifts on his feet and adds, "There was something else, though."

It feels like the answer is right in front of us, just out of reach. We can't help it—Kath, Ingrid, and I all lean forward.

Pete opens and closes his mouth. Then he says, "But I'm not supposed to tell anybody."

I picture a star expanding, growing brighter and hotter, waiting to explode. I struggle to hold my frustration in. "Pete, Jennifer's missing. Can you please *try* to help?"

Pete looks at me as if I've sprouted fangs. "You don't have to get so mad."

He has no idea how hard I'm holding back my anger. He has no idea how loudly I want to yell. "Tell us," I insist.

Pete looks at the three of us like he's calculating his odds of escaping. Then he sighs. "A couple weeks ago, she asked me if I could help get her into the local radio station. So I did."

I turn to my friends. Kath's eyes go wide, and Ingrid—who's been attempting to camouflage against the wall—stands a little straighter. Nowhereville's radio station is located inside the mall, which is only about a fifteen-minute drive from here.

"If Jennifer got into the station," I say, "that probably means she succeeded in contacting aliens."

I don't even bother hiding this from Pete. Right now I'm too excited to care.

"Um, okay," Pete says after a moment of awkwardness. "Anyway, I figured she might have gone back there, so I went to the mall the day after she ran away, and I thought I saw her, but then she was gone. I looked through the security footage to double-check."

"You went through the security footage?" Kath asks. *"How?"*

"The mall cops know my dad. They like me." Pete shrugs. "We went through the tapes for a while, and then we saw this girl on the film, and I told the guard, 'Stop the tape! That's her!'"

"Oh my god," I whisper.

"Right." Pete nods. "But when the guard paused it, it wasn't Jennifer. It was some other Japanese girl."

Ingrid winces. Kath groans. The burning star inside me grows hotter. A moment of hope, smashed because Pete can't tell Asian people apart. "She's Chinese," I say. "We're not all the same."

Kath raises a brow at me, and it takes me a second to realize: I don't think I've ever talked about being Asian before. My cheeks flush, and I wait for the embarrassment to follow, but it doesn't.

Pete raises his hands. "Whoa, I know *that*. I just really thought I saw her."

I grit my teeth. I kind of don't know why I'm so mad.

Ingrid clears her throat. It's the first time she's spoken

in a while, but she squares her shoulders and says, "Okay. Okay. You didn't see her on the tapes. But back to the radio station . . . what exactly did she do while she was there?"

"I don't know. I waited outside while she went into an empty sound booth and fiddled with the control panels. She said she was interested in the tech." He pauses. "Do you think that had to do with her running away?"

I don't even bother to state the obvious *yes*. "How did you get in?"

Pete lifts one shoulder. "My dad is friends with the owner of the station, so I know a lot of the people there. They like me."

Kath takes a very deep breath. "Do you have any idea how easy your life is?"

Pete grins. "You just gotta be friendly. Crack a few jokes."

"Yeah, if your dad is the *sheriff*." Kath looks like she might murder him—which would be a problem, considering *sheriff*—so I interrupt.

"Excuse us for one moment," I say, before grabbing Kath and Ingrid by the wrist and pulling them out of the stairwell.

Kids bustle around us in the hallway. Normally, everyone would ignore us, but today a few of them glance our way and whisper to one another. Tess has already spread the word, it seems.

I ignore them.

"I don't trust Pete," I whisper. "But if he can actually get us into the station, that might be the only way to find Jennifer."

Kath nods. "Agreed."

Ingrid wraps her arms around her stomach. "It was just . . . really bad with Pete last year. I don't want him to start up again. . . ."

I know what she means. Pete's scary.

But then I think of Jennifer and her aliens, and the world expands out into the universe, with its infinite stars, infinite galaxies, infinite space. When you think about it like that, Pete is so infinitely small.

"We won't let him do that to you," I promise. "And Pete is so small in the grand scheme of things! He only has power if you give him power." The revelation makes me giddy.

But Ingrid's eyes flash with annoyance. "He's not small compared to *me*. I didn't *give* him any power. Some people just have it. Pete has it because his dad's important, and he has a lot of friends, and he's . . . tall? And if you're unpopular, he'll use that power to make your life miserable."

I hesitate. I know he used his popularity to make her miserable. I know he did that to other people, too. But there are also things I don't know. Like, do some people really just *have* power? Or is it given, or taken, or some combination of both? Surely some people have to follow in order for others to lead.

And then I wonder: How many followers does it take to make a leader? And what if someone decided not to follow? Would that even matter—or would there just be somebody else, waiting to fill the space?

I swallow. This is the problem with intellectual curiosity. It makes things messy.

"If you don't want to involve him, we can figure out another way," I say. "We'll go to the radio station and I'll cause a distraction by shouting about aliens, and you two will sneak in, and we'll find Jennifer on our own."

Kath gives me the tiniest nod, and I feel my shoulders relax.

Ingrid glances toward the sky. Then she sighs. "Fine."

Without waiting for our response, she pulls the door back open to find a confused and antsy Pete. She takes a deep breath. "All right. Get us into that radio station."

((((((22))))))

Pete presses the doorbell to the station and buzzes us in.

"Follow my lead," he says, all obnoxious kinds of confidence as he swaggers up to the front desk.

Kath, Ingrid, and I asked Mom to drive us to the mall after school today, and because she's still so happy that I might have new friends, she agreed without asking too many questions. Pete met us there, since he lives only a few minutes away, and now we're at his mercy, relying on him to get inside.

Pete flashes a smile, and the woman at the front desk melts. "Hey, June. Remember that project I was doing for English last week, about observing a workplace?"

Her brows pinch with concern. "You were with Jennifer Chan, weren't you? How're you holdin' up?"

"Not great. I'm worried about her." To my surprise, Pete sounds genuine, and I start to think he might actually care about Jennifer.

June nods. "We all are, hon. We've been putting out messages on the radio, and I've texted my cousins all through the state. I've got a big family and we're all looking. We're all praying. And she'll come home safely. We don't let people get hurt here in Norwell."

I chew my cheek.

"Right." Pete clears his throat, looking a little shaken. "But, um, for the project, I was wondering if my other group-mates could observe, too?"

"Of course, sweetie. Happy to help." June stands, gesturing for us to follow. "Would you like to speak to one of our radio hosts?"

Too quickly, Kath says, "No, no."

When June's smile falters, Pete clears his throat. "The project is more about *silently* observing, not interviewing. We want you to forget we're even here."

Somehow Pete's charm works, and June's suspicion fades. She sets us up at a small table by the coffee maker. "You just enjoy your observations over here, now. As long as you don't touch anything, you're golden." To Pete, she adds, "And say hi to your daddy for me."

I can actually *feel* Kath suppressing an eye roll, but it works. June walks away, everyone else is busy, and nobody pays us any attention. I thought a radio station would be more dramatic than this, but it's kind of just an office. A mostly empty office.

Scanning the space, I spot a sound booth in the corner. It's barely big enough for the four of us, but it's got a radio panel, it's empty, and that's all we need.

"There," I say, pointing.

166

"That's perfect," Ingrid confirms.

Pete clears his throat. "June *did* tell you not to touch anything."

Kath sighs. "Now is not the time to dabble in morality, Pete."

He snorts. "Okay. Chill."

We don't really want Pete here, but we also don't know how to get rid of him, so we don't say anything when he follows us into the booth.

Kath and Ingrid sit on the two seats in the booth, and Pete and I hover awkwardly behind them. Right away, they get to work. Kath presses buttons and twists dials, doing everything June told us *not* to do, and Ingrid pulls out her phone, researching the best way to send a message into space.

"I need silence for a minute," Ingrid murmurs as she frowns at her screen. Her left fingers tap the table restlessly, and I can tell she's wishing for earplugs. I always thought the earplugs were a weird Ingrid thing, but now I get it. Sometimes the sound of other people's opinions is so loud that you can't even hear yourself think.

"What are they doing?" Pete whispers.

"Quiet," I respond.

He's quiet for about ten seconds. "So nobody's gonna explain what's happening?"

"Quiet," Kath repeats.

He shakes his head. "This is so weird."

I'm frustrated. I'm scared. I'm a burning star. "Do you ever feel bad?"

He blinks at me all dramatic, like I am the *most confusing person on the planet*. "About what?"

"About being a bully." It's not something I'd normally ask, but I guess I'm not normal anymore.

And, well, Ingrid finally gets her silence, because nobody even breathes.

I glance at Ingrid, and though her back is turned to us, her shoulders are stiff.

Pete looks at Kath, like he actually believes she might be on his side.

She raises a brow. "I mean, you are."

He laughs. "You guys are crazy."

"What about the capoeira thing?" I press.

Pete lifts his shoulder into that perma-shrug. "We were just having fun."

"At Jennifer's expense." I don't know what I'm expecting him to say or what I even want from him.

"Look, everyone has all these opinions about Jennifer now, like she's fragile or something. My dad says stuff about how she must have been under a lot of pressure from her mom, or she must have been a troubled kid. And people at school are saying all kinds of things. But I don't think she's like that. She kinda let stuff roll off her, and we were friends after the capoeira thing. I didn't mean anything bad by it—unlike you, by the way."

Nausea rises. "What?"

"Oh, come on. With those photos?"

I swallow. "How did you know about that?" I flick through

my memories. It was only *us*. Reagan, Tess, and me—our group chat. Nobody was supposed to know.

But of course, Jennifer found out, and I didn't know how.

Kath winces and says, almost gently, "Everyone knew, Mallory."

I glance over at Ingrid for confirmation, but she's frozen, every muscle tensed. She doesn't deny it, and my stomach sinks.

Turning to Pete, I ask, "Did Reagan tell you?"

He shrugs a yes.

"And are *you* the one who told Jennifer?"

It was wrong of us to do it, of course. But it was also wrong of him to tell her. More wrong, possibly. It was cruel just for the sake of being cruel. I want to lunge over and shove him.

"Okay, calm down." Pete holds his hands up. "I didn't tell Jennifer anything. I don't get involved in stupid girl drama. Girls are always talking behind each other's backs and tearing each other down, and that's just not what I'm about."

"Would you just SHUT *UP*?"

I picture a star exploding—and for a second I almost think it's me, a burst of light and heat.

But it's actually Ingrid who's spoken. She's standing, hands gripping the table. Even she seems a little stunned by her voice, but she presses on, forcing the words through clenched teeth. "That is *exactly* what you're about, Pete. You don't get to tear me down at school and then say that about *girls*. I am just. So. SICK of you."

Kath's eyes go wide, and she murmurs, *"Dang."*

I want to see Pete's reaction, but I can't pull my eyes off Ingrid. These past few days, I've seen how much Pete's bullying changed her. This whole time, I've assumed that the new Ingrid was worse—a tamped-down, scared version of herself.

But this is part of the new her, too. And she definitely isn't scared.

When I finally turn to Pete, he blinks like he's noticing Ingrid for the first time. Then he takes a step back. "Look, I'm not the bad guy here. I want to find Jennifer just as much as you do. But I didn't sign up to get attacked. All I've done is help you, and if this is how you respond, I'm out."

He pulls the door open and says over his shoulder, "But just so you know, June's pretty nosy, so you might want to hurry. She'll probably check on you at some point." Then he walks out without even bothering to close the door.

After a few moments of silence, Kath says, "Well, the radio's all set up, and now I guess we need a lookout. I volunteer."

When Ingrid and I kind of . . . hesitate, a smile ghosts Kath's lips.

"This will be my redemption," she deadpans, "even if I have to make do without a walkie." Then she steps out of the room and adds, "Ingrid? That was awesome. You are awesome."

Then

23

Jennifer wasn't supposed to know about the photos, but somehow she found out.

Two weeks after it started, Reagan, Tess, and I were standing by Reagan's locker before school, and Jennifer appeared, practically out of nowhere.

She was standing with her fists clenched and her chin tilted up, like she was strong and proud, even though she was shaking. That would have been bad enough on its own, but that wasn't the worst part.

The worst part was her hair.

She'd gotten it cut exactly like Reagan's, with the straight-across bangs—only they didn't look good on Jennifer. They made her face look even rounder. And of course, Tess had already sent three secret pictures to our group chat.

"I know what you're doing," Jennifer said. I watched her dig her fingernails into her palms, and I winced.

The haircut didn't make any sense. I mean, why would she copy Reagan? Why would she copy Reagan and then *confront her*?

Tess said, "Nice hair, Jennifer."

Jennifer flushed, but she didn't look at Tess. She didn't look at me, either. She looked right at Reagan. "I know what you're doing," she repeated.

I imagined Jennifer staring at herself in the mirror that morning, repeating the line over and over until she got it just right. *I know what you're doing.*

I wished she'd come to me before involving Tess and Reagan. Maybe we could have worked it out quietly. Instead, a confrontation like this felt horrible and awkward for everybody. Why would she put herself through that?

"Okaaaay," Reagan said, drawing the word out. Her lips quirked up, hinting at a smirk. "What exactly am I doing?"

"Someone told me you're taking pictures of me. Without my consent."

Reagan snorted. "That's a little dramatic, J."

I glanced at Tess, wondering if she knew anything about who told, but she looked just as surprised as I felt.

Jennifer inhaled sharply. "What's your problem? Why are you so *mean*?"

"What's *my* problem? You're the one getting worked up over nothing." Reagan looked at us for backup. Tess laughed. I just stood there.

Jennifer did this weird, unhappy laugh. Her eyes were wide and wild, and she looked nervous but almost giddy, too—like this confrontation was both terrifying and thrilling. Jennifer was different now. It was like we'd changed her.

"It's not nothing," she said. "I just want to know *why*. Why do you hate me so much?"

172

"Jen-ni-fer," Reagan said, enunciating each syllable, the same way Pete had just a few weeks ago, in front of the school. "Nobody hates you. You think the whole world revolves around you, but the truth is, nobody *cares*."

I wanted to disappear.

Jennifer stared at Reagan. "Are you really just a terrible person?"

Reagan's Shark Eyes flashed.

I wanted Reagan to disappear. I wanted Jennifer to disappear.

I stepped forward and told Jennifer, "You should just leave. This won't end well for you."

I was trying to help.

But Jennifer looked at me and spat, "You're a coward." Then she turned and walked down the hall, so fast she almost ran.

As soon as she was out of earshot, Tess grinned. "Right. *She's* the one running, but *we're* the cowards?"

Reagan's jaw twitched, like she was grinding hate between her teeth. "The *nerve*. Did you see her hair?"

"Just let it be." My voice sounded funny, like it was coming from somewhere far away.

"She *copied* me," Reagan said. "First she steals Pete. Then she steals my hair? Honestly. Who does she think she is?"

"I don't think she *stole* Pete," I said.

Tess's eyes narrowed. "Whose side are you on?"

I looked up at her. Tess was four inches taller than me, which I usually forgot about, but right then I felt small in comparison. "I'm on Reagan's side. Obviously."

"I feel like that's not actually obvious?"

I bit my lip.

"Like, you don't seem very loyal? Because Jennifer just attacked Reagan and you don't even seem annoyed. You just seem sad?"

"I am sad," I said. "For everyone."

"For *us*," Tess corrected.

Reagan rolled her eyes like my loyalty bored her—but I could see the tension on her face. "Jennifer's so *exhausting*. She invents all these lies to make her life sound more exciting than it is, because she can't handle reality. That's just . . . pathetic."

I thought about Reagan's mom and the lie Reagan created—which made me feel disloyal. When I met Reagan's eyes, she looked away.

"It's all an act," Tess agreed. "You know, her fake I'm-so-quirky thing? Like she's different?"

I couldn't deny the uneasiness growing inside me. Everything had escalated so fast—I didn't even know how it had happened. *I* was exhausted. Reagan and Tess—they were being exhausting.

"Maybe she really is different," I said. "Maybe Jennifer just has a different attitude. That's just *her*, with the capoeira and the aliens—"

I clamped my lips shut, attempting to swallow my words. But it was too late. Tess's eyes popped. "Wait. What?"

"What?" I repeated, as if I could erase the last ten seconds.

"Aliens," Reagan said slowly, like she was savoring the word.

Tess laughed. No, Tess *glowed*. She bubbled with joy.

Tess always reacted like this to a new piece of gossip. "Oh my god, stop. You said aliens. What, does she commune with aliens or something?"

"Tess, don't."

I felt Reagan's eyes on me, and when I looked up, she squinted, trying to read my face. "Why are you protecting her?"

"I'm not," I snapped. "I just . . . don't know for sure, is what I mean. So I don't want to start rumors that aren't true."

"Of course not," Tess agreed.

Reagan's voice was quiet, almost gentle, almost . . . desperate. "Mal, best friends don't keep secrets from one another."

I thought about those late-night sleepovers with Reagan, the way they'd always felt so safe. But we'd been having fewer and fewer of those lately. Jennifer had changed everything.

Their eyes burned into me, and I mumbled, "Jennifer believes in aliens—but it's not as weird as it sounds. She has whole notebooks full of evidence. It's actually kind of—"

"*Evidence?*" Tess's brows shot up.

Reagan's eyes narrowed. "Honestly, that's kind of creepy. Who would *want* to believe in aliens? Some slimy space creatures watching our every move? No thank you."

"It's like God," I blurted. Reagan and Tess stared at me.

Tess cleared her throat. "Um . . . no, Mallory. It's not like God. It's actually not like God at all?"

"Right." I didn't know why I'd said that. "That's not what I meant."

"God makes people feel *comforted*. He makes people feel like there's a bigger picture. Aliens make people feel . . ." Tess shuddered. "Squicky, Mal. They make people feel squicky."

Reagan nodded slowly. "Squicky. That's what she is. That whole confrontation was squicky."

"I don't think—"

Reagan cut me off. "We can't let her win. We need to teach her a lesson."

Everything in me emptied out. I felt hollow.

And then Reagan asked, "Where does she keep those notebooks?"

Jennifer Chan's Guide to the Universe
Volume VI, Entry No. 4: Dark Energy

Have you ever heard of dark energy? Me neither, until
today.

Basically, all the stuff we understand about the
universe only makes up ten percent of it. Stars, planets,
molecules, and atoms—all that is just a slice of the
cosmos.

The remaining ninety percent is made of dark energy,
which isn't the most accurate name, because it's not actually
dark at all. It's invisible. Unknowable. We don't understand
what it is or how it works.

All we know is that it makes the universe expand.

If it were up to gravity—one of the few things we're
<u>sure</u> we're sure about—the universe wouldn't expand at all.
It would actually contract until it implodes, because gravity
wants to pull everything closer together. Dark energy, on the
other hand, pushes everything apart.

Scientists describe the universe as a tug-of-war, and
right now dark energy is winning.

It's a little wild, if you think about it. Because even
though aliens are nothing to be afraid of, when I think about
dark energy, I get shivers all the way to my toes.

What if there is something scary out there? Imagine! We

go out there, expecting to contact nice aliens, but what we find instead is a mysterious, invisible force. A force that's more powerful than gravity itself. And there's nothing we can do to control or understand it.

We're all just at its mercy.

Now

(24)

Soon after Kath closes the door, the radio bursts to life with static, and Ingrid looks up at me. "This is it. Are you ready?"

I stare at the panel, like an alien might actually bust out of it. There's a special dial for the frequency, with a Sharpie line drawn at 180 megahertz. A handwritten label reads: *DON'T GO PAST THIS NUMBER.*

At 1420 megahertz, we've gone past it, just a tad.

"Do you think this will break it?" I ask Ingrid.

"I'm sure it'll be fine," Ingrid says, though she sounds less than sure.

"What do we do now?"

Ingrid tugs at her cross necklace. "I haven't had much time to figure this out, but I think we can say a brief message, followed by some mathematical codes. Obviously, it's unlikely they'd understand us, but they'd probably understand *math,* considering those principles are consistent throughout the universe."

"Right." I lean into the microphone and clear my throat. "Um, hello? Aliens? Jennifer? Um, we come in peace."

"Okay." Ingrid nods, looking a little uncertain. "That's a good start. Now I'll just send out a few numbers in the Fibonacci sequence." She finds a button she likes and taps it, pressing out a series of signals.

"Do you really believe aliens will know what the Fibonacci sequence is?" I ask, as someone who definitely doesn't know what the Fibonacci sequence is.

"Up until this afternoon, I didn't even believe in *aliens*," she says. "But Fibonacci spirals occur all over the place in nature, and even in galaxies, so it might be the closest thing we have to a universal language."

We stare at the radio panel, but all we get is static.

"What about . . . Is there a way to send beeps?" I ask. "Like, three beeps?"

Ingrid searches the panel for a button she likes and presses it. *One, two, three.*

Static.

I feel a headache pulsing behind my eyes, and Ingrid turns the volume low, so the static is just a hum in the background. "Let's give it a minute," she says. "We know there's a delay."

I nod. We wait. These minutes last so long you could stuff entire galaxies into them.

And Ingrid says, so quietly I barely hear her over the static, "How did Jennifer do it?"

I think she's talking about contacting aliens until she says, "He started off bullying her, like he did to me, but she turned it around. She made him like her. *Like*-like her. And I'm not saying I wanted that, but all the stuff with Pete made me feel so small. How did she . . . become big again?"

"I don't know." I'm wondering, too. Jennifer had a way of making people like her.

Staring at the radio, Ingrid says, "I was so mad."

I nod, though she's not looking at me. "Pete was awful."

"No," she says. "I was mad at everyone. I was mad at *you*."

The air kind of goes out of the room. "But I didn't participate in any of that. I didn't do anything."

"Exactly." Ingrid's hands press into the table, like she wants to smash it into the ground. "I know we weren't best friends, but we were still *friends*, right? And then when everyone was being mean to me, you didn't *do* anything."

I swallow. Here it is, finally: the reason she hates me. It's not because I got popular. All I can do is blink as the revelation settles over me. "But nothing I did would've stopped them."

Ingrid pauses. "I've been doing a lot of research on aliens," she says, as if this isn't a total subject change. "There are a lot of people who believe that unidentified aerial phenomena might actually be extraterrestrial."

"I saw that in my research, too," I say cautiously. I'm not sure where she's going with this, but maybe she's decided that focusing on the aliens is more important than our history.

"But even then, those people think UAPs might be alien *drones*, rather than actual aliens visiting. And even if aliens *are* visiting us, not many people think they'd get involved in human life."

"Jennifer does," I say. "She thinks aliens are coming to

help us. Because if they've worked so hard to get here, why wouldn't they get involved?"

"Maybe they're afraid of us," Ingrid says, still staring at the staticky control panel. "Or they think interfering would do more harm than good. Or they don't believe they're powerful enough to make a difference."

"But of course they're powerful enough. They're way more technologically advanced than us."

"Well, then maybe they just don't care enough to do anything, and everything else is only an excuse."

Ingrid turns to pin me with her stare, and I finally get it. *Right.* This is the problem with having smart friends. You think they're talking about science, but it turns out they're making a point.

The situation at school was way different from a UAP, though. Because of course I didn't have as much power as literal *aliens.* How much difference can one human possibly make?

But also . . . maybe there's some truth to what she's saying. Maybe I didn't consider Ingrid enough. And I didn't consider Jennifer enough. Maybe I didn't care enough to do enough.

How many followers does it take to make a leader? And more than followers—how many people who just turn away and say nothing?

I rest my hand on the table as dizziness clouds my senses. The world is out of ratio, like it's too small or I'm too big, and suddenly all I want is to run out of this room and bury myself in my bed. It would be so much easier to forget this conversation, this search, the Incident, all of it.

But I tell her, "I should've said something."

Ingrid snorts, a sound that's almost goofy—but it's angry, too. "Yeah, okay, Mallory. I'm not mad anymore. At least, not as much. But a little bit, I guess, I am. I don't want to be."

Suddenly her voice is so thick with emotion that I think she's going to cry. "It's not fair because I was so *happy*. I was so happy and I don't *want* to be angry. But it sits there now, inside me. I don't know how to get rid of it."

"I'm sorry," I murmur.

She takes a shaky breath. "In church, they're always talking about forgiveness, and I know I should forgive Pete, but I don't know how. I don't know if I can find that in me." She closes her eyes for a long heartbeat. When she opens them again, she says, "But I think I can forgive you."

My heart somersaults. I feel like I'm not doing enough or saying enough right now, but it's so awkward and so intense, and there's no guide for this. "Thank you."

She turns back to the radio panel. Still static. She's quiet when she says, "Pete wasn't the one who told Jennifer about the photos."

I shake my head, feeling lost. I'm still processing her hurt. Why is she defending *Pete*?

When it's clear I don't understand, Ingrid says carefully, "I did."

It takes a second for my brain to catch up with my ears.

And then stars dot my vision. Betrayal slices through me, so quick and unexpected, though I'm not sure I have the right to feel it. "But *why?*"

Ingrid tugs at her necklace. "I felt like telling Jennifer was the right thing. People at school were talking about what you guys were doing, and I felt like she had a right to know."

"Oh." I feel like I'm underwater and can't find the way up. "Maybe . . . you're right?" I can't tell good from bad anymore. I have no idea.

"*No*, Mallory." Her voice is full of fire, like she's thought this through and she believes what she's saying, wholly. "Jennifer didn't know you guys were being mean, and I told her. She never had to know that. She never had to *feel* that."

I wish, so hard, that we never took those photos in the first place. Regret weighs me down, as heavy as gravity.

"I told myself I was trying to help her because that's what I wanted people to do for me," she continues. "But now I don't know. Now I think . . . maybe I just didn't want to be the only one anymore. The only angry person."

"You're not the only angry person," I say. It feels like more of a confession than I meant it to.

She looks at me, and as her expression softens, she nods. It's the tiniest of movements, but I know what it means. *Thank you for seeing me.*

"Just don't tell Kath it was me," she says.

I think about my conversation with Kath, how Kath didn't want to be friends with Jennifer, and she didn't want me to tell Ingrid about it. I think about the secrets I'm keeping, about the Incident.

How many people carry secrets like this? How many people secretly hurt each other? Because Ingrid and Kath are good, and if *they* hurt people . . . maybe humans really are just bad. Maybe we can't help but hurt one another.

The thought makes me so sad that I have to close my eyes.

And then I hear a beep.

My eyes fly open.

Another beep.

Ingrid and I lean forward.

Then, *beep-beep-beep-beep. Beeeep-beeeep-beeeep. Beep-beeeep-beeeep.*

The radio goes silent for a moment. Then it repeats.

"It's a pattern," Ingrid breathes.

"Ingrid," I gasp, trying not to squeal. "It's *working.*"

She scrambles to take notes, and I'm so excited I practically levitate. We're going to find aliens. We're going to find Jennifer.

And then Kath's knock interrupts our celebration.

Ingrid and I stare at each other, eyes wide.

"We have to go," Ingrid says.

She's being smart and logical, and of course we should go. But *not now.* "What about the code?"

The radio *beep-beeeep*s. *Beep-beeeep-beep*s.

Ingrid scribbles in her notebook.

And then the door bursts open. It hits me in the back and I stumble forward.

When I turn, I see June, her hand clasped over her mouth. "What—?" she sputters. "I told you kids . . ."

She pushes past us to turn the radio off, then steps back, looking surprised and disappointed and also a little bit . . . sad. "I'll need to call your parents."

25

Mom's mad.

As I sit at the kitchen table with my parents, Mom keeps closing her eyes and inhaling.

"I didn't realize not yelling required so much oxygen." I don't mean for it to sound so sassy, but it comes out that way.

Dad sighs like, *Here we go.*

Mom is not amused. "I don't know what's going on. But this lying and sneaking around is not okay. It isn't you."

I inhale, an angry breath of my own. "How would you know? How would you know who I am?" My voice cracks over the last word, and I realize I want an answer. I want her to tell me, because maybe I don't know who I am, either.

Mom leans back, blinking quickly. "I'm your mother. Of course I know you."

Dad takes her hand and says to me, "Mallory, you can talk to us."

They don't understand that I *want* to talk to them. I want to tell them about Jennifer and the alien hunt and the

Incident. I want to ask them for help and let them carry this weight.

But how can I do that when they already look at me with so much disappointment?

"Please," Mom begs.

"We . . ." *We got a code from aliens. We need to find Jennifer. We're so close. That day, in the bathroom, the Incident—*

My parents lean forward, and I start over. "I know it was wrong to use the radio without permission. But we need to get back there. It's important."

Mom frowns. "Why?"

"I can't tell you why. You just have to trust me."

Dad rubs a hand over his stubble. Mom sits very still. I let myself imagine how they might help. I picture them taking me back to the radio station and telling June, *We're very sorry, but there's been a misunderstanding. Our daughter needs to use your radio. Here, have some pie.*

Mom lets out a very long breath. "That's not good enough, Mal."

The air goes out of my lungs. I blink away the unexpected sting in my eyes. "But, Mom—"

"But, Mallory," Mom says, voice firm. "You have to *talk* to us. Trust goes both ways."

"Yeah, exactly!" I explode. "And you don't trust me!"

Dad interjects, "Mallory, watch your tone."

I gape at him. He's usually on my side, or at least neutral, but now it's two against one and I have nobody.

"We're trying to trust you," Mom says. "But you have to give us a reason."

"*That's* not good enough." When I jump to my feet, my chair goes crashing to the floor. "I'm your daughter. That should be the reason."

Shaking hard, I run to my bedroom and slam the door behind me.

I lean against my bedroom wall and let myself sink, sliding all the way to the floor. My blood feels too hot and I can't cool down and I'm so uncomfortable that when my phone buzzes in my pocket, I'm grateful for the distraction.

It's Ingrid, requesting a video call. When I accept, I see her, sitting fully clothed in what looks like an empty bathtub. Kath is already on the line, lying on her stomach in bed.

"I figured out the beeps and decoded the message," Ingrid says, not bothering with hello. "It's Morse code."

Kath raises her brows. "Morse code? How do the aliens know *that*?"

Ingrid bites her lip. "I was wondering the same thing. But it makes sense when you consider the delay. If radio waves take years to travel through space, it's possible that the aliens are just now receiving our very early radio signals. Which, of course, were often in Morse code. It's *possible*—though still unlikely—that aliens have learned to communicate with us that way."

I imagine aliens listening in on us, way up in the darkness of space, and I shiver.

Kath tilts her head. "Okay, so what does it say?"

" 'H-O-W,' " Ingrid reads, consulting her notes, " 'A-R . . .' and that's it. That's all we got before June interrupted us."

I sit up a little straighter. "So that's 'How are . . .'?"

Kath nods, her screen shaking. "Yeah, but that doesn't help much."

"We need to get back to the station to hear the rest of the code," I say.

Ingrid pulls her legs to her chest and rests her chin on her knees. "I don't think I can do it. My mom's not thrilled with me, and I don't think she'll let me go back there. I had to hide in the bathroom just to call you."

Kath winces. "My parents aren't too happy, either. And June's probably banned us from the station for life."

I run a hand through my hair. We've decoded half of an *alien message,* and yet, because we're kids, there's nothing we can do about it. That's so frustrating I can hardly stand it. I have to hear the rest of that message.

But I also know that Kath and Ingrid have already gotten in enough trouble for this. I can't involve them anymore.

"You're right," I tell them. "But . . . thank you for everything. I really, really couldn't have done this alone."

It sounds a little too much like a permanent goodbye, and I don't want it to.

Kath must hear that, too, because she says firmly, "Of course you couldn't. Ingrid and I are brilliant."

I laugh, trying to mask my relief.

"Yom Kippur starts tomorrow night," Kath continues, "and I have to spend the holiday with my family. But this is still a priority. Let's figure out our next step at school to-morrow."

After they hang up, I stare at my blank screen, thinking about one hundred billion galaxies with one hundred billion stars—until a knock on my door startles me, and I drop my phone to the floor.

"Yeah?" I say.

I'm hoping for Dad, but it's Mom who peeks her head in. Dad probably went out to help the search party for a couple hours. My parents have been alternating shifts for the past few nights.

"Can we talk?" Mom asks.

I don't want to, but I nod.

She opens the door wider. "Can I turn the lights on? It's so dark in here."

I shrug, but she doesn't turn them on. I wonder if part of her wants to walk in and rest a hand on my shoulder, like she used to—but she stays in the doorway.

"Your dad and I . . . we do trust you," she says. "You're a good kid."

"Okay," I murmur, too uncomfortable to look at her.

She pauses. "I know you're going through a hard time with Jennifer. But we're here for you. I'm here for you."

"I know."

"Okay, well . . . I love you."

Even though I want her to leave, I also don't want this conversation to end. I'm thinking about our fight, and sud-denly I need to know who she thinks I am.

191

It's not like I can just ask that, though, so instead, what tumbles out of my mouth is, "Do you think I'm Korean?"

Maybe the question is close enough. *What do you see when you look at me?*

That awkward moment with Pete pops into my head, when he confused Jennifer with another Asian girl, and I got mad, and nobody really knew how to react.

"Of course I do," Mom says, surprised, as if the question never crossed her mind. Then she adds, "Do *you* think you're Korean?"

She looks almost nervous, like she's afraid of the answer, which makes *me* nervous. "It doesn't really matter what I think," I say.

Mom frowns, her hand still on the doorknob. "Of course it does."

She's starting to get intense. I can feel it. She's going into Mom Mode, where everything's a debate and she's always got a point to prove. I'm starting to regret bringing this up. "Yeah, of course," I repeat.

"Mallory." She hesitates before taking a step toward me. "Why wouldn't it matter what you think?"

I take a deep breath. I wanted answers, not questions—but I know Mom well enough to know she won't let this go. "I just meant . . . well, we're all just a collection of what other people think about us. So, yeah, it matters what I think. But what *other* people think matters even more."

A crease forms between Mom's brows. "Who told you that?"

I pause. I never thought of the idea *coming* from some-where. But when I pull through my memories, I find Reagan and me, curled up in bed during one of our million sleepovers.

You can control who you are by controlling the way people see you, she'd said.

Mom sighs. Shrugs and sighs are our language, mostly. "Mallory . . ." Another step forward. "*You* decide who you are. Nobody else."

I fight back frustration, because I don't want every con-versation with Mom to end in anger and annoyance. "Okay, but . . . it matters if people think you're a good person or a bad person. You're the one who always says it matters how we treat people."

"That's exactly right. Life isn't about what people think. It's about what *we do*. It's about the impact we have on the world."

"Right." What would she say if she knew about the Inci-dent? What would she say if she knew about my impact?

Mom opens her mouth to say something else, but I inter-rupt her. "I'm really tired."

She swallows her words before nodding. "It's late. Get some sleep."

She leaves me in the dark of my room, and when I hear my parents go to sleep, I climb out my window again, just to look up at that infinite sky. Why would aliens come so far, just for us? If they're not planning to interfere, what are they looking for? What are they trying to learn?

I imagine them asking questions I don't know how to answer.

How are you?

Who are you?

Who do you think you are?

Jennifer Chan's Guide to the Universe
Volume VI, Entry No. 36: Expanding

A fact about the universe is that it's always expanding. Thanks to dark energy, infinity is growing even more infinite, and all the galaxies are moving farther away from one another.

If I set up a massive telescope right here in Chicago, it would look like all the stars in the universe were running away from me—which wouldn't be exactly right, of course. It's not personal.

A fact about me is that I ran away last week.

It was just for a couple of days, and I hid in a neighbor's shed. I told Rebecca it was because I missed Dad, but the truth was, I just needed to get away from her for a while.

With Dad gone, it's obvious how different we are. She wants me to stop talking about aliens. She wants me to start thinking about how I dress. She wants me to try harder with the kids at school.

I just couldn't take it anymore.

But after I came home, she was so upset, and I felt so bad that I couldn't tell her any of that. She was talking about moving, as if it were Chicago that caused all our problems, rather than Dad dying and everything falling apart.

At first, I tried to convince her not to, but then I thought: yeah, maybe a fresh start would be nice. And in that fresh start, I don't want to be the kind of kid who scares her mom like that.

So, I'll do what she wants. I'm not going to stop hunting for aliens, but I can make compromises. If she wants me to wear certain clothes and get popular haircuts, that's not a big deal. I can do that. I can try harder.

I swear, right here in this guide to the universe, that I'm gonna change. I'm not gonna be a person who runs away anymore.

Now

26

The next morning marks four days. Officially longer than Jennifer's ever been away before. Officially the time when adults are getting very worried.

Hearing her name on the news (*missing, missing, still missing*) nearly launches me into that panic hole again. The news anchor talks about the search party and the police investigation, and she mentions gators and all the wildlife that may have hurt Jennifer, which makes my breakfast crawl back up my throat.

In the final segment, they interview Ms. Rodgers, from school, who says she's decorating her house with twinkling lights, to make the night a little brighter for Jennifer, wherever she is out there.

The whole thing makes me dizzy, but I can't give up. I just need to find the rest of the code.

At school, Ingrid texts, asking if I know a private place to meet during lunch, and though I'm wary of involving them more, I suggest the basement bathroom in the chapel. Guilt swirls in my chest, as if bringing them there is somehow a betrayal of Reagan, but that bathroom is exactly what we need. Nobody will interrupt us there.

I get out of class a little early, so I head to the bathroom before Ingrid and Kath. But when I push the door open, someone's already there, curled in a heap on the floor.

After a handful of panicked seconds, I realize it's *Reagan*. And she's crying.

My chest lurches, and without thinking, I rush over and sink to the floor beside her. She's crying. Reagan is *crying*.

I'm not proud of the swoop of fear in my stomach—the same feeling as leaning out over the Ferris wheel and seeing the ground so far beneath me. And there's a part of me that almost feels *betrayed* by Reagan. As if, by showing her fears so openly, she broke some kind of promise, some unspoken rule of our friendship.

"It's okay. You can talk to me. You can trust me," I tell her, wanting it to be true. "I've got your back."

She struggles to find words, and when she looks up at me, her eyes are red. "People are talking about us, Mal."

I pull back. I expected her to be crying about Jennifer. I thought, underneath it all, she felt the same way I do. "What do you mean?"

"Well, it started with Tess telling everyone that you're best friends with Kath and Ingrid now and that you've created some Jennifer-obsessed, alien-worshiping cult."

I try not to roll my eyes. "That's obviously not true."

"And now people are talking about *me*," she continues.

"They think Jennifer running away was my fault, because of the pictures. Everyone thinks I'm a bad person. But it's not . . . it's not my fault."

She says it like a promise, or a prayer. If I asked her to, she'd say the same thing about me. *It's not your fault.*

"Reagan . . . ," I say.

"Do you think I'm a bad person?" Reagan looks at me with such desperation, like she needs me to say no.

"No." I'm surprised to find that I mean it. I wonder if I should. I wonder what Kath and Ingrid would say.

Reagan sniffs.

"And it doesn't matter what people think." I repeat Mom's words, though they don't feel quite right. It mattered to Ingrid. It mattered to Jennifer. It might have even *changed* them. Jennifer said that what people thought made no difference to who she was, but I don't think that was totally true.

"You don't believe that," Reagan says, seeing straight through me.

And I remember what it's like to have someone know you so well that it's impossible to hide. Jennifer wrote something in her notebooks—how when people are abducted, they don't run. They stand right in front of the UAP, and they can't escape, not even if they wanted to.

I think I get that. Getting abducted by aliens must feel kind of . . . nice. Kind of like the aliens *picked* you. And how cool and amazing and out of this world is that? To feel like someone incredible wants to be with *you*. They saw you and thought you were worth something.

Maybe, before that, you didn't think you were worth anything at all—until someone leaned forward during PE and whispered, *Follow me. I have a plan.* And maybe that's the biggest thing that ever happened to you, to be seen, to be picked, to be understood and accepted.

Or at least—that's how I imagine it might feel. It's just a theory.

"I don't know what I believe," I tell Reagan. "I don't know if we're good people or not. I'm just . . . I'm afraid we did something really bad, with the pictures and with . . . with the things we said in this bathroom. I'm scared we can't ever make it okay."

The words from that day seem to echo off the bathroom tile. The crack in the wall seems to widen.

Reagan shakes her head. "So that's it, then? We're just the bad guys now?"

I swallow. "I don't know."

Reagan swipes at her tears, jaw hardening. "Do you even care that there's a meteor shower tonight?"

My breath catches in my throat. She told me about it a few weeks ago, and I know how much she dreads those falling stars, stained with the memory of her mother. But with everything that's happened, I forgot.

She nods like she's just confirmed a fundamental truth. "Apparently I'm not important to you anymore. You probably think I deserve to feel this way."

"Reagan, you know you're important to me."

She says to the crack in the wall, "You told me you

wouldn't leave, but of course you did. As soon as things got hard, you ran off with Kath and Ingrid and completely abandoned me."

"I'm not running off," I say. "Reagan, please."

My emotions are a broken compass. They spin in all directions: sympathy for Reagan, guilt for forgetting, anger because her tears almost seem like an excuse, desperation to fix our friendship, and then all the way back to guilt. I shouldn't be worrying about her while Jennifer is still out there.

I'm torn between my new friends and my old—the new *me* and the old—but maybe I can bring all of this together somehow.

I lean forward. "Kath, Ingrid, and I are going to find Jennifer. We're so close."

She blinks, lost, and I take her silence as encouragement to continue. "And maybe finding her will make up for the things we said to her. Like . . . it balances out the universe."

Reagan frowns. "Seriously? Tess said you were still looking for her, but I didn't want to believe that."

"Remember when I said I saw something in the sky? There have been more signs, too. There was a message on the radio. And the assembly—that wasn't just Principal Vaughn messing up the microphone. That was a 'Wow!' signal. There's something going on, Reagan, and it's bigger than us. You can help. You can be part of this, too."

She pulls away, and I realize she's angry with me. "Mallory, Jennifer's gone. She either ran away or something worse. And it happened right after . . ." She gestures around us, to the tile, the sinks, the scene of the crime. "Honestly, what if you don't like what you find?"

"What do you mean?"

She doesn't even flinch when she says, "I'm not sure looking for her is worth it."

Even in her anger, those words surprise me. I reach for her again but stop myself. "You're sitting here crying about what we did to her, but as soon as there's a chance to make it better, it's not *worth it*?"

Reagan's voice is scary in its blankness. "I'm trying to protect you. That doesn't make me a bad person."

"Protect me from what? From Jennifer?" I laugh in a way that isn't funny. "Reagan, she's not the bad guy. Pete's a jerk. She didn't *steal him away*. She didn't *copy your hair*. She didn't do anything."

Except, as I say it, I wonder if it's true. Jennifer *did* do something. She went searching for the secrets of the universe. And she stood up for herself, for the way she saw the world.

"This was never about *Pete*," Reagan says, emotion bleeding back into her words.

"Then what was it about?"

When Reagan turns back to me, her eyes are made of ice. She doesn't answer my question. I didn't really expect her to. Instead, she says, "I'm trying to protect you from the possibility that something terrible happened to her."

Fear clouds my senses. I don't want to imagine the worst.

Beneath Reagan's ice, there's something hot and burning.

For a second, I think she's going to cry again. For a second, I think she'll change her mind, that she'll help me find Jennifer after all. For a second, I think she wants to.

Then she stands up and slings her backpack over her shoulder. Without a word, she walks out.

When the door swings back open, I think it's Reagan,
changing her mind. Despite everything, I know she must
want to make things better. She's just afraid.

But it's not Reagan who enters. It's Kath and Ingrid.

I scramble to my feet, trying to shove all those mixed-up
Reagan feelings aside.

"Well, this bathroom is incredibly spooky," Kath says.
Then she looks at me, and her brows furrow. "And you look
awful."

"I feel awful." My honesty kind of surprises me, but I
guess I don't have the energy to hide from them.

"Me too," Ingrid says. "My mom's not happy, but she's
used to this. You know, like our old hijinks."

I never thought of it as *our* hijinks. To me, they were always Ingrid's. I assumed Ingrid thought of them as hers, too.

Something flickers over Kath's face, something close to
jealousy, but none of that's important right now. Right now I
need to focus on Jennifer.

"So I was thinking," I say, "if going back to the radio station isn't an option, I have to find another way to get the code. I'm going to do it on my own, so you don't have to worry—"

Ingrid interrupts. "Mal, I told my mom what we were trying to do."

I feel an immediate rush of envy, because I wish I could be honest with my mom without worrying.

Then the reality of her words hits me. Ingrid's mom knows. Which means she'll try to stop us. "What? Why'd you do that?"

"Not, like, the *whole* thing, with the aliens and the journals, but about trying to find Jennifer. We talked about how Jennifer's run away before, and . . . my mom made some good points."

"Some good points," I repeat.

"Just that . . . maybe this doesn't have anything to do with aliens." Ingrid speaks quickly. "Maybe she ran away because of the bullying, because of those photos and stuff."

"But—" My voice breaks. I rest a hand against the tiled wall. "But it can't be just that. What about all the alien evidence? What about the UAP I saw? And the Morse code on the radio? And the assembly thing?"

Kath winces, and Ingrid shakes her head.

"I was thinking about that, too," Ingrid says. "But what if the lights were from a search party? What if the Morse code was just a random person's signal that we picked up? What if the assembly was an awful prank?"

Kath looks like she's going to be sick.

"That doesn't make any sense," I say. I hear the wild edge in my voice, but I can't pull it in. "The assembly wasn't a prank. We heard the 'Wow!' signal."

Ingrid's expression slides into something dangerously close to pity. "I'm just saying . . . What if it wasn't aliens?"

When Kath speaks, her voice is very small. "It wasn't."

Both Ingrid and I turn to her, and she looks at the floor, like she wants to disappear. Softly, she says, "It was me. The assembly was me."

Jennifer Chan's Guide to the Universe
Volume VI, Entry No. 52: Where Are You?

I'm trying to be patient, but the aliens are taking a long time
to find me.

I'm waiting, but waiting isn't easy in a world where I
don't always fit. It isn't easy when Rebecca tries to make me
fit. And I don't know how much longer I can wait for aliens
before I go and find them myself.

28

"What?" It's the only response I can manage. The *Wow!* signal wasn't aliens. It wasn't otherworldly or cosmic or religious. It was just , . . . Kath?

"But—why?" Ingrid sputters. "Why did you do it? Why did you *lie*?"

Kath looks like she wants to cry. "When Mallory first told us about the UFO thing, I thought she was just making up stories and being a jerk. But the more she talked about it, the more it seemed . . . possible."

I stare at her, totally stunned. Behind her, the crack in the tile seems ready to swallow us up. Bizarrely, I almost feel like laughing.

I believed I was a good person. Wrong. I believed there was something more out there. Wrong. I believed I could make a difference.

Why are people so afraid to believe, Jennifer? Well.

"But, Ingrid"—Kath turns to her best friend—"you were so upset with Mallory that you wouldn't even listen. And I just thought—I *knew*—that if you did listen, if you really believed there might be aliens, you'd be able to find them. You're just so *intense,* in the best way. You'll do anything to figure things out. I mean, you basically set Howard Park on *fire* because you were curious about wildfire control."

"*Park* is generous," Ingrid says automatically. "It's more of a giant field. And it was a very small fire."

"Not the point," I say.

"You're right." Ingrid nods. "Let's get back to the part where Kath lied."

Tears pool in Kath's eyes, threatening to spill. "I'm trying to make amends. Yom Kippur is the Jewish Day of Atonement, so I've been thinking about the way we hurt others, on purpose or by accident or because we were trying to help and it totally backfired, and I'm figuring out how to make it right."

I inhale, exhale.

Kath speaks so fast she's almost tripping over words. "I know I shouldn't have lied, but I'm so sorry. Please. Forgive me."

Ingrid shakes her head, stunned. "But I don't get it."

"I was really scared," Kath says. "Jennifer was gone, and I was worried that something bad happened to her. Or that something bad *might* happen to her. And I just kept thinking, I don't know, maybe if she had real friends here, she wouldn't have left. Maybe if I hadn't avoided her and told her the Science Club was full, she'd be here, with us. Maybe it was my fault she left."

"It wasn't your fault," I whisper, because even though I'm feeling confused and angry and betrayed, I know it wasn't.

"You pushed her away?" Ingrid asks Kath.

Kath nods miserably. "I didn't want you to be a target again."

Everything is spiraling in a way I can't control. Nothing is what it seems. Nobody is *who* they seem. Ingrid hid the truth about telling Jennifer about the pictures. Kath hid the truth about pushing Jennifer away—and, apparently, about the assembly.

I don't know what's real anymore. I don't know what to believe.

But I grab on to something I know for sure. Jennifer disappearing wasn't Kath's fault, and no matter what they might think of me, I can't let my friends carry the guilt. I can't keep hiding the truth.

I take a deep breath. And I tell them about the Incident.

Then

29

Reagan said, *We have to teach her a lesson.* And so we did.

It wasn't meant to be so bad. But Reagan was getting angrier, and I figured, let her get this out of her system. Jennifer was pushing and pushing, and I thought we could show her how things worked.

I thought it was the better of two evils. The alternative was letting Reagan stew, and the war would have gotten worse the longer things stayed below the surface. This was the only way to stop it.

Reagan, Tess, and I got to school early that morning so we could go over the plan.

"Are you sure we won't get in trouble?" Tess asked, twirling a strand of her hair. We were standing at our usual spot by the lockers, watching as students trickled into school.

Reagan rolled her eyes. "Why would we get in trouble? We're literally just gonna talk to her."

Tess nodded. "Totally. I'm all for the plan. But, like, what if she tells a teacher?"

"Tess," Reagan said. "Are you seriously scared right now?

Because if you're scared about something so small, I don't know how I can be friends with you."

Tess's eyes grew wide.

"Kidding. Obviously. But you're being ridiculous." Reagan ran her fingers through her bangs. "This is serious. Jennifer's head is getting way too big, and she's becoming a monster. We have no choice but to stop her."

I swallowed as Reagan turned to me. "Mal, don't you remember the way she spoke to you? You are *literally* the nicest person I've ever met, and she said you're evil. That's just *beyond*."

Honestly, I didn't really know if Jennifer was mean to me. Every time I tried to play back the memory of Jennifer confronting us, the details got fuzzier. The more we talked about it, the less I could recall.

But I did remember how it felt. The way she'd looked at me gave me heartburn—I could still feel all her negative thoughts about me, worming their way through my chest like maggots.

"I don't think Jennifer understands how things work at this school," I said. "We just need to tell her so she can stop upsetting people."

Tess sighed. "Please. Jennifer *definitely* knows how things work. She's trying to get all the power for herself so she can basically *overthrow* us, you know? She's out of control. Mal, you're being way too nice."

Reagan smiled at Tess, a kind of smile I hadn't gotten from her since school started.

Tess grinned, puffed by Reagan's attention. "So, are we going to slay this beast, or what?"

Reagan turned to me. "Mal, do the honors."

Half of me wanted to run away, but the other half wanted to see this play out. I wasn't sure if that was intellectual curiosity or something much worse.

I took a breath and texted Jennifer: Can we talk?

She texted back almost immediately: Not really. You're not the friend I thought you were.

It was like she'd punched me in the throat. The words, they were basically an act of violence.

I read her text out loud.

"See?!" Tess yelped. "She's totally out of control."

"Tell her it's about aliens," Reagan said.

Tess laughed, but there was nothing soft or humorous about Reagan. I should have seen her Shark Eyes and stopped.

But . . . Jennifer hated me. Reagan, on the other hand, accepted me without judgment. And I was *tired*. I was tired of questioning myself, of second-guessing, of worrying so, so much. I was tired of holding back.

I texted Jennifer: I'm serious. I think I saw a UFO last night.

Reagan read over my shoulder and snorted. "Perfect."

Jennifer responded, Are you messing with me? Unidentified aerial phenomena are not a joke.

Tess leaned over, too. I wanted to push my friends away. But there was also a part of me that needed them close.

"Wow, she's actually crazy?" Tess said, and laughed.

Not joking, I texted back. Meet me during lunch in the basement bathroom under the chapel.

Jennifer took a while to respond. On my screen, I could see her typing and deleting and typing and deleting. I imagined her expression, that hopeful grin spreading across her face.

But I shook the image out of my head. Probably she was just angry. Probably she hated me and thought I was a terrible person. If she already believed that, what did it matter if I proved her right?

Jennifer sent her reply: Okay. I'll be there. I'm trusting you.

She had no idea how much trust could possibly hurt her.

((30))

Reagan, Tess, and I sprinted to the basement bathroom as soon as the lunch bell rang. It's an unspoken rule between us that we never, ever run, because running anywhere outside of a track or a running trail makes you look desperate and weird—but for this, we made an exception. We had to get there before Jennifer.

Panting, grinning, carelessly sweating, we exploded through the bathroom door. "Hide, hide, hide!" I whisper-shouted, pushing them into a stall.

We laughed as they crammed in, laughed so hard our sides cramped.

In that moment, everything was funny. It felt like a game, like none of this really mattered. We were powerful. We were the most powerful girls in the whole grade. Everybody knew it except Jennifer, and now she would, and then nobody could touch us. Nobody could take that power away. I felt dizzy, and for once, I didn't run from the feeling. I let it eclipse me. The world was small beneath my feet, and I could do anything.

As Tess and Reagan huddled in their stall, giggling and shushing, I leaned against the sinks, trying to look casual.

The light flickered. That fluorescent light was always flickering.

Jennifer took a while to get there. At one point, I thought she wasn't going to come at all, and I felt mixed up about that. Relief and anger and a little bit of disappointment.

But she did come. She opened the door and slid inside, finding me there, seemingly alone. Her shoulders loosened and she tested a smile. "You really saw a UAP?"

I nodded a little too eagerly. "Yeah, totally," I lied. My voice didn't sound like my own. It sounded like Reagan's almost, when she was making fun of someone.

I cleared my throat.

"Where?" Jennifer asked.

I hadn't thought this far in advance. I had to improvise. "Out my window last night."

She dropped her backpack on the floor and hoisted herself onto the ledge of the sinks, kicking her feet back and forth. "What did it look like? What did it *feel* like?"

"Um . . ." When were my friends gonna come out? How long would they let me lie? I tried to remember what Jennifer had said about UFO sightings. "Lights? I don't know. I didn't feel anything."

She thought for a moment, and I worried she was on to me—that she'd point and say, *Gotcha*. But she said, "Were the lights red or white? There's been mixed messages in the alien community recently. Some people think there are actually two UAPs competing for our attention, but I think it's just one. There are plenty of things to account for something looking different to different people. The clouds, for one, and the other lights in the sky. Not to mention confirmation bias, which—"

The bathroom stall banged open, and Reagan stepped out, followed by Tess.

"Heeey, Jennifer," Reagan said, her voice sick-sweet, dripping with a cutesy, casual kind of hate. In her hand, she held Jennifer's notebook—Volume VII, the one Jennifer had trusted me with.

Jennifer froze. She blinked rapidly, *onetwothree*. This was not the same girl who'd confronted us. Then she'd been ready. Now we'd caught her by surprise.

Reagan pouted. "What's wrong? I thought you were brave. I thought you weren't afraid of us."

Tess grinned and shook out her curls. The two of them stood on one side of the bathroom. On the other side, Jennifer slid off the sinks and pressed herself back.

I stayed right in the middle. I couldn't even move, to be honest.

I wouldn't move, to be more honest.

Reagan stepped forward and Jennifer flinched, as if Reagan had physically hurt her. And I wondered if Reagan *would* hurt her. We'd made this vague plan, but we'd never discussed what would happen now. We thought of it as a hypothetical: *What if we taught Jennifer a lesson?*

We never considered what that lesson would be.

Jennifer stood, backed up against the sinks, face pale. Her eyes darted toward the exit.

She could have run. But she turned back to Reagan—to *us*. Her voice shook. "What do you want?"

"*What do you want?*" Tess mimicked.

Jennifer bit her lip.

"You have an ego problem," Reagan said. "And we're here to bring you back to Earth. Right, Mal?"

When I'd told Reagan that Jennifer needed to come down to Earth, I'd meant it as a joke. At least, I thought I had. It didn't seem so funny now.

Jennifer turned to me, eyes wide, and I didn't know what she wanted me to do. What could I do?

"I . . . ," I murmured.

Reagan held the notebook up and flipped to a random page. " 'I'm always hoping for more, and I'm going to find it. I'm going to change the world,' " she read, her voice as thick as poisoned honey. "Isn't that cute?"

Jennifer looked at me, then back at Reagan. "Please," she said. "Give it back."

Tess stuck out her bottom lip. "Is brave little Jennifer begging? Is brave little Jennifer scared?"

This was pointless. And mocking, and *mean*. I didn't know what I'd expected, really, except that maybe we'd show Jennifer how the world worked. We'd explain that there were unspoken rules you had to follow, and then she'd know better. She'd learn that you had to protect yourself because nobody was coming to save you.

But this didn't feel right.

"We don't have to read from it," I said.

Jennifer wouldn't look at me. I could practically feel her ignoring me, erasing me with her mind.

"I'm not scared," she said, but her voice wobbled. "I just want my notebook back. I'm trying to be mature."

Reagan's eyes flashed. That was the absolute worst thing to say to Reagan, especially when she was in Shark Eye mode. She held up the journal. "Oh, and it's *mature* to think you can change the world? Do you really think you matter? Do you really think anyone cares what you have to say?"

Reagan ripped the page and tossed it to the floor. Jennifer made a strangled noise.

Flipping to another entry, Reagan read, "'I'm going to prove everyone wrong. I'm going to stand in front of the non-believers and say, *Look at me. Look at everything I can be.*'" Reagan ripped it again. *Rip, rip, rip.* She tossed Jennifer's words to the floor. "So, what are you gonna say now? We're waiting."

Jennifer opened her mouth, but nothing came out. She'd learned capoeira for self-defense, but how could she defend herself against an attack like this?

Reagan ripped another page, the sound of torn paper slicing through the bathroom, echoing off the walls. She passed the journal to Tess, and Tess ripped pages into pieces. "'They're going to find me,'" Tess read. Then *rip, rip, rip.*

Horror wrung my stomach. Moments ago, I'd felt powerful enough to stop Jennifer. Now I felt powerless to stop us.

Tess passed the journal to me, and Reagan raised a brow. It was a reflex, really, taking the book. It landed in my palms with a thud, infinitely heavy, though most of the pages were already littered across the tile floor.

"Mallory," Jennifer whispered.

The whole notebook was already in shreds. It was already unsalvageable.

And my relationship with Jennifer? That was unsalvageable, too. What difference did it make, any of it?

I ripped a tiny corner.

Jennifer made a noise that didn't even sound human.

I felt everyone's eyes on me, and that journal in my hands—that *journal*. I'd only read a few of the entries because I couldn't handle it—Jennifer writing about who to be and how to be as if she had the answers.

Jennifer didn't have to question. Reagan didn't have to question. They knew who they were, and they knew how the world worked. And it seemed so unfair that some people just *knew*.

I tore another piece. And then another. I felt possessed. Like I wasn't me. Or maybe this was me and I just didn't know it.

I thought back to when Jennifer called me a mean girl, and I wondered if she hadn't just *thought* that—if, maybe, she'd *seen* it. I wondered, too, about the difference.

The book was too heavy. I dropped it.

And Jennifer's face changed. Something broke inside her, her hope hollowed out.

Reagan shook her head. "Who do you think you are, Jennifer Chan?"

Jennifer didn't respond, so Reagan answered for her. "You think you're special. You think you're better than us because you're so *different,* so *quirky.* Because you have big dreams and beliefs, and someone, at some point, told you that you could actually achieve them." Reagan's voice broke, and she swallowed. "But I see through you."

Jennifer's whole body shook. She was vibrating. And she wouldn't look at me. Her eyes darted again toward the door. Then she pushed away from the sinks, unsteady on her legs, and ran out of the bathroom.

"Go on!" Tess shouted after her as the door swung shut. "You'd better run." And then she laughed, like this was all a joke.

But Reagan stared at me. My heart pounded in my chest. My hands shook, and I wrapped my arms around myself, grabbing my elbows. We'd put Jennifer in her place, and the universe was back in order. Maybe this was how the world worked. But maybe it wasn't how the world *should* work.

I turned to the empty space where Jennifer had stood, but all I saw was myself in the mirror, looking frightened, panicked, hopeless. I closed my eyes.

"Well," Reagan said, oblivious to my shattering world. "I don't think she'll be bothering us anymore."

Jennifer Chan's Guide to the Universe
Volume VI, Entry No. 31: A Question

Sometimes when I'm lying awake at night, I like to prepare interview answers for when I'm famous and everybody wants to know my story.

News reporters will shove questions and microphones into my face, and I'll hold up my hand, all glamorous, and say, "One at a time, please."

"What's your secret?" they'll ask. "How did you discover aliens and save the human race?"

"I have to thank the people who supported me," I'll say, and everyone will listen. They'll be hanging on to every word. "If you want to believe in impossible things, you have to find the people who believe in you."

Now

31

A weird thing happens when you see something with your own eyes—when you *participate,* when you do something wrong—and nobody ever talks about it again. The less you hear about it, the more you tell yourself it never happened at all. You can shove reality into the shadows of your mind, so it's always lurking but never fully present. You're afraid of your own memory. You're afraid to believe it.

And then one day it emerges from the shadows. And you don't know how to face it.

After telling Kath and Ingrid about the Incident, I am shaking. I already know they won't want to be friends with me anymore, but that doesn't stop the slice of pain when I see horror roll across their faces.

My shoulders curl in, like if I make myself small enough, I can disappear. "I know it was wrong."

"Wrong," Kath repeats, like she's tasting the word and it's sour.

"Really wrong," I add. Only it sounds like a question.

Ingrid shakes her head. "You listened to my story about showing her the pictures and you saw my guilt, and you just . . . let me keep it."

I look to Kath, hoping for an ally, but she's still staring at me like she has no idea who I am.

"I'm still mad at Kath," Ingrid says. "But you. What you did was unforgivable."

My throat tightens. "It all just happened. I wasn't thinking."

"But you were," Ingrid bites back. "Of course you were. You're always thinking. About how you look, about how people see you, about who's popular and who's not. You thought about this. You knew the consequences, and you didn't care."

I choke on my words. "I didn't know she'd run away."

Kath takes a step back from me. "But you hurt someone. For fun."

"No," I protest.

"We were helping you," Ingrid says, "and you lied to us."

"I didn't lie." I just didn't tell the whole truth.

Ingrid points at me. "You told us Jennifer ran away because of aliens. But she didn't. She ran away because of *you*."

My ears ring. My vision clouds. My heart leaves my body, and I'm somewhere way up, far, far into the universe. From space, our sun looks as small as a grain of sand.

And then, too soon, I come crashing back to myself. My body prickles with sweat. My intestines slither and snake.

I thought Jennifer needed to know the way of things. I thought she needed to follow the popularity food chain and fit herself into it. And the horrible, worst truth of all:

I thought, after so much time spent worrying, I deserved a moment of power. I thought taking hers was the only way to get it.

Maybe people are afraid to believe because believing the wrong thing has devastating consequences.

She ran away because of you.

"So I'm just the bad guy now?" I ask, hating the words even as they leave my mouth.

Ingrid doesn't respond. She storms out, and as Kath follows, she turns to look at me one last time, staring like she wants to say something, but has no idea what.

32

The world is ending.

I wanted to believe. I wanted to find something out there, something bigger than me, something that would explain away what happened with Jennifer and fix it.

But I was silly to think I could be someone who believed.

I can't make it through the rest of the school day, so I go to the health center and tell Nurse Lila I have cramps.

I haven't done this since that first day with Reagan, and I expect her to turn me away, but her brows pinch. Maybe it's the look on my face. Maybe it's the way my hands are shaking. Or maybe it's just the effect of Jennifer's disappearance, the way it's made everyone a little softer. Because instead of giving me an Advil and sending me back to class, Nurse Lila nods and says, "You can rest on a cot for a bit."

"Thank you," I say, voice wobbling.

"Hang on."

I stop, worrying that she's changed her mind. I can't face my friends right now. I don't even know if I *have* friends right now.

But she slides her desk drawer open and hands me a Hershey's Kiss. "Chocolate always helps." There's something in her eyes that tells me she knows this isn't about cramps.

I take the chocolate, wanting to cry because I don't deserve her kindness. But I blink back my tears and thank her again before curling up on a cot.

I spend the rest of the day at the health center. Every hour, Nurse Lila comes in and asks if I'm ready. Each time, I shake my head, and she leaves a chocolate on the edge of my cot.

My parents pick me up at the end of the day, full of a worry that only grows when I answer their questions with empty-hearted grunts.

At home, Mom stops me before I escape to my room. "You can talk to us," she says. "Please."

I want to. The truth is so close to the surface that I'm afraid if I open my mouth it'll tumble out. But then I remember the way Kath and Ingrid looked at me. I shake Mom off and run to my room instead.

I come out for dinner, only because I'm worried my parents will actually combust with concern if I don't. Also, because I skipped lunch.

As we sit at the table, Mom takes a deep breath, and I know she's gearing up for a speech. I brace myself.

"Mallory, honey, you've been so withdrawn lately—for the past couple years, really—and I'm telling myself that's normal. I'm trying to give you space. But we just want to be your parents. We want to be here for you."

"I'm okay," I lie. "I just don't feel well."

I don't meet her eyes because I'm afraid of what I'll find there. Strain settles over us as we eat Dad's sauerkraut, and I notice the anxious glances Mom and Dad exchange over my head.

They let me finish my meal in silence, but when we're done, Mom walks to the oven and pulls out a pie. The scent of cinnamon apple puffs off the hot crust, and when Mom sets the pie on the table, she looks at me with a mixture of desperation and love.

"I'm okay," I repeat. And then I burst into tears.

Dad jumps to his feet as if the house is on fire, and then, not knowing what to do, he sits back down and grabs my hand.

Mom runs around the table and kneels beside me, wrapping me in her arms.

I don't wait for them to ask again. I tell them everything. I tell them about the alien hunt and our Jennifer investigation. I tell them about the Incident. I tell them about Reagan crying in the bathroom, and Kath's and Ingrid's reactions to my confession.

It's the second time I've talked about the Incident today. It's the second time *ever*. This time, it feels less like an

Incident and more like a slow build of mistakes—one stacked on another, a dangerous, unsteady tower of regret.

I climbed that swaying tower without realizing how high I'd gotten. How did I let it get so far? Why didn't I look down to see what we were doing? I imagine the tower crumbling. I imagine myself crashing down.

"Do you think I'm a bad person?" I whisper.

"My god," Dad murmurs. It's a lot to process. "Of course not. Did you do something wrong? Yes. But you're trying to make amends. You're learning from this."

"I learned that I can't trust myself."

Mom makes a pained noise. "I told you before that what matters is how we treat people, and that's true. But I wasn't clear enough, because when I say 'people,' I don't only mean friends and family and strangers. I also mean *you*. How you treat yourself matters. And you have to be kind enough to forgive yourself when you make mistakes. You have to trust yourself to fix them."

I let her words wash over me, trying to believe them.

Mom tucks a strand of hair behind my ear, and Dad squeezes my hand. "Do you know why Catholics practice confession?" he asks.

I swallow. "So God can know how bad you are?"

"What, no!" He frowns. "My interpretation, at least, is that it helps us see who we are. Confession isn't about telling our secrets to God. God already knows. It's about revealing our true hearts to ourselves, because we can't know who we are when we're hiding from who we've been."

Mom gives him a small smile. "There's truth there whether

229

you believe in God or not," she says. "We learn to do better when we face our shortcomings. It's a painful process. Some people never do it. But you are. And we're proud of who you are and who you are becoming."

My breath catches. My throat hurts.

"You're doing the right thing by telling us," Dad says.

I stare at the table, studying the grooves of the worn wood. "Will I always have to choose between doing what's right and doing what feels good?"

Mom hesitates. "Doing what's right doesn't always feel good in the moment, does it? Sometimes it can feel really scary. But there's this feeling after, when the person you are and the person you want to be match. It's like . . . peace. Do you feel it now?"

"Maybe?" I look up, and when I see their expressions, full of pride and strength and understanding, something in me shifts. The always-there ball of worry in my stomach starts to loosen. My chest opens up.

And as their words rumble through the new open space of my heart, something slides into place. The truth is right in front of me.

"And, Mallory?" Mom adds. "No more investigating. Please."

I nod, but my brain is whirring. *We learn the truth when we face our mistakes.*

Maybe aliens aren't out there—but Jennifer still is. And there's still one last journal, the one I've been avoiding because it was too horrible to look at what I did.

Finally, I have to face it.

33

I wait for my parents to go to sleep, and then I pull the crumpled plastic bag out from under my bed. After Reagan and Tess left the bathroom, I stayed behind and salvaged what I could of Jennifer's journal, and now, as I dump the contents onto my floor, the universe seems to tilt.

Ripped pieces of paper burst from the bag, tiny scraps of cruelty falling to the ground like shooting stars. *Jennifer Chan's Guide to the Universe, Volume VII.*

Jennifer's looping handwriting stares up at me.

Wincing, I reach for the ripped pages, then spread them out like a mosaic of all Jennifer's hopes and dreams and secrets and discoveries.

I attempt to piece her words back together. It's a mess, and I keep flashing back to that moment in the bathroom. *Rip, rip, rip.* My vision goes fuzzy and I close my eyes.

Then, remembering something Jennifer did, I turn my palms to the sky and start to exhale in short bursts. *Whoosh-whoosh-whoosh.* It looked so weird when she did it, but I get it now. It's centering. I can do this.

I open my eyes to the task in front of me, and an hour later, I have paragraphs pieced together, all across my floor. I finally read what Jennifer wrote—the words she asked me to read months ago.

Here is Jennifer, with all her heart, and seeing her fully feels a little like skin peeled back, emotion scraping against something raw. I feel what she feels, and knowing that I hurt her . . . hurts.

I'm desperate to stop, but I keep going, and as I slide yet another scrap of her handwriting together, two words catch my eye. *Crop circles.*

I have a sense. A feeling.

Frantic now, I search for the matching pieces, and when I find them, I see that she's writing about a field in Nowhere-ville. A field where she saw crop circles. A field that made her believe.

My heart hammers with the hint of a hunch, and I tug through my memories, searching for the answer. When I slept over in her yard, Jennifer mentioned seeing crop circles before, over near the military base. And right next to the military base is a park . . . a park that is honestly more like a field, the same one Ingrid and I burned our initials into, three years ago. Wobbly lines that might have looked, to a hopeful girl driving by, like crop circles.

Understanding floods my veins, hot and cold at once. The message on the radio wasn't *how are*. It was *Howard.* Howard Park.

I think back to that night with Jennifer and I remember

something else, something she said about meteor showers being good for alien hunting. There's even a radio tower at the park—something that never seemed important until this moment.

And I know: Jennifer's going to be at Howard Park. Tonight. During the meteor shower.

I scramble for my phone, which tells me that the meteor shower is just before 2 a.m., in a little over an hour.

So how do I get there?

I jump to my feet and run to my desk, where I rummage for Ingrid's three sheets of paper. Flipping them over, I read: *METHOD, MALAISE, MESSAGE.*

Method. I could bike, but that would take way too long, and it's too dangerous at night.

I could ask my parents to drive me. It's only twenty minutes by car. But Mom just told me to stop investigating. They'd send me back to bed, worried, and I don't have time to convince them otherwise.

That leaves one other option. I know who I need to ask. I just don't want to. I take a breath—a chance—and I text Reagan.

Call me.

We're not "call me" friends. When we weren't at school or sleeping over, we'd text. But this situation is beyond texting. And I know, somehow, in that best friend way, that Reagan's awake right now—that she's staring at my message on her phone, deciding whether she wants to listen.

Please, I type. With a pretty cherry.

While I'm waiting for Reagan, I move to *Malaise*. What gives me a bad feeling, besides everything? I'm worried about driving, but Reagan's confident. She knows how to do it. So that's a risk I'm willing to accept.

But there's something else nagging at me. I steel myself again, and this time I call Kath. I won't ask for help, but I feel like I owe her and Ingrid an update. After everything we've been through, I don't want to do this without telling them. And I think Kath, unlike Ingrid, will pick up.

When Kath doesn't respond on the first call, I call again. It goes to voicemail, so I call again. And again.

It's no use. Either she's asleep with her phone on silent or she's ignoring me.

Malaise flutters in my chest—and then I catch sight of something, pushed to the corner of my desk. A plastic brick.

I pick up the walkie-talkie. The chances that Kath has hers in her room are small. And the chances that she left it on are even smaller. But . . .

"Kath, it's me. Mallory. Please pick up," I say into the walkie-talkie. And then, after a moment, I add, "Over."

I stare at it, willing it to respond.

It crackles.

"What's wrong with you?" Kath's voice demands. "It's past midnight, and I'm *mad* at you, Mallory."

I breathe out a hot rush of emotion. *Whoosh*. Because even though she's mad, at least she's talking to me.

Then she adds, very reluctantly, "Over." And I could cry.

"Kath, I figured it out," I rush to say.

Kath pauses. "What do you mean?"

I tell her about Howard Park and the journal pages and the meteor shower. My words tumble over each other, and when I finish, there's a rustling sound before Kath speaks. "How do we get there?"

I'm not sure I heard her right. "No, Kath, you don't need to go. I'm going. I'm asking Reagan—"

"*Reagan?* You're asking *Reagan* and not me?"

"You wanted nothing to do with me!" I say. "And I get that. I was just telling you because—"

"Because we're in this together. Even though you did a terrible thing and lied about it. And now you're trying to leave us out?"

"I wasn't . . . I just . . ." I bite my lip.

She sighs. "At services tonight, the rabbi talked about forgiveness, how it's not only between you and God. He said God exists in the relationships between people, so forgiveness is between you and the person you hurt. And I'm not really sure if I believe in God, but I do believe in fixing things when you're sorry. It's work."

"That's what I'm trying to do," I tell her.

"I know," she says. "And even though I am *mad at you*—let's not forget—there's a part of services that goes, 'May all people be forgiven, because all people are at fault.' I have my own amends to make with Jennifer. So . . . let's do the work."

"Should I call Ingrid?"

Kath hesitates. "She's really angry, at both of us. So let me tell her. Over."

While I'm waiting to hear back from Kath, Reagan calls.

"Mal? Are you okay?" Her voice is clear and sharp, wide awake, and even now, even after everything, there's that spark in my heart. She called, so maybe things between us are not broken forever.

"I know you said it wasn't worth it," I begin, before I can second-guess myself. "But I know where Jennifer is. She might be in trouble, and we have a chance to help."

Reagan hesitates—one second, two. "Why are you telling me this?"

I've never been so nervous to talk to Reagan before. I force myself to speak, force the words out, clear and strong. "Because I think you want to do the right thing. And I need your help. I need someone who can drive."

Jennifer Chan's Guide to the Universe
Volume VII, Entry No. 73: Believe

Even if you become a world-class alien hunter, you might still have moments of doubt. That's normal. It happens to everyone. It even happens to me.

It's true: sometimes even I wonder if I'm wrong to believe.

Sometimes I see lights in the sky, and I think: What if it's not a UAP after all? What if it's just a passing plane? Or a satellite? Or something from the military?

Sometimes I think about Area 51, the place that made so many people believe, the place that turned a military weapons compound into a symbol of hope. On the worst days, I wonder: What if the strange things people see aren't aliens coming to save us? What if they really are just bomb tests and weapons? What if everything we've been seeing has just been human violence all along?

These past few days, moving from Chicago to Norwell, have been some of the worst days. I've been fighting with Rebecca. I've been missing Dad. I've been afraid of all this _new_.

But whenever I feel like that, I remind myself: I'm excited about this move. Florida's cool. It's the state with the second-most UAP sightings in the country. It's home to Cape Canaveral, the launch site for space shuttles. And most importantly, it's our fresh start. So this place is special.

And on our drive to our new home, we passed that field, the one I saw crop circles in all those years ago, and I got that something-bigger feeling—the belief that everything happens for a reason. I think I'm meant to be here.

((((34))))

I sit outside on my front lawn, letting the sprinkler-soaked grass dampen my jeans as I wait. There's electricity in the air, but the sky is clear. I haven't thought much about Ingrid's third *M, Message.* I don't know what I'll say to Jennifer, but I'll figure that out when we get there. And we have to get there—fast.

I check my phone: meteor shower in thirty-eight minutes.

I check my phone: no new texts or calls.

Since Kath insisted on coming, too, we made a plan for Reagan to pick Kath up first—and maybe Ingrid, if Kath can get through to her. Then they'll all drive to my house. But they were supposed to get here fifteen minutes ago.

I call Kath. Straight to voicemail.

I call Reagan. Straight to voicemail.

It occurs to me that maybe they bailed. Maybe I'm all alone.

And then my phone buzzes with a text from Kath: Relax. We're coming.

I place my head between my knees and tell myself to breathe. Only Kath would tell me to relax at a time like this, but somehow it's comforting.

And just when I'm bursting with the waiting, I hear Reagan's dad's gray van, stuttering down my road. It start-stop-start-stop-start-stops until it finally slams to a halt in front of the house.

I jump up and run to my friends. Reagan's sitting in the driver's seat, face pinched with concentration and annoyance. Kath is lecturing Reagan about something, but I can't make out her words from outside the van.

I throw the passenger door open, my lungs squeezing like they can't get enough air.

"Reagan can't drive to save her life," Kath informs me. "And I mean that literally, which is alarming, considering she's driving us."

"I *can* drive. I'm just a little rusty." Reagan rubs her temples. "I'd like to see *you* drive, Kath."

"I can't drive, Reagan. *You're* supposed to be the one who can drive. That's the whole reason you're here."

I interject before Reagan can respond. "It's okay if you're rusty," I say, though I'm not sure it is. I was so confident in Reagan's abilities that I didn't consider how dangerous this might be. "Go slowly and safely. Nobody's on the road this late."

Turning to Kath, I add, "Ingrid didn't want to come?"

Kath's face falls. "I talked to her, but I don't think she's ready to see either of us."

I force a nod, though it aches. Kath, Ingrid, and I only

had a temporary alliance, but it felt so close to real friendship. I didn't realize until now how badly I wanted that.

"Thank you for coming," I tell Kath.

"I want to believe in goodness," she says.

Reagan stares ahead and grips the steering wheel so hard her knuckles turn white. "Well, you needed me, so I'm here." Her lips press into a line. "You ready?"

I nod. "I'm glad you're both here. This is scary, and Jennifer's probably scared, too. She's out there alone."

Kath takes a breath. "She won't be for long."

Reagan looks back and forth between us, her brows pinched like she's seeing something strange. Finally, she says, "It's good. That you care."

I can tell she's being genuine, but there's something unsettling about her tone. Something I don't quite get. "I know you care, too," I say.

I can't tell if she hears me. She rubs her arms, brushing her goose bumps away. "Let's go."

I almost wonder if there's something more I should say, but there's no time. I hoist myself into the back seat as Reagan flips on her blinker. She glances out the back window to reverse, shifts the van out of park, and then slams her foot on the pedal.

Unexpectedly, we lurch forward.

My stomach flips and Reagan yelps, but instead of shifting from Drive to Reverse, she panics and slams the gas even harder.

The van speeds forward and hops the curb of my front lawn.

"REVERSE," I shout.

"BRAKE," Kath screams.

And then we're all screaming as the van goes slamming into my mailbox.

As we jerk against our seat belts, the post splinters into a million pieces, then falls to the ground with a crash. I'm so rattled that I think my internal organs might have turned to goo.

Reagan rips the key out of the ignition, and the engine makes a terrible noise before stopping.

We stare at my mailbox—or at least, the mangled remains of my mailbox. None of us can even speak.

Finally, Kath says, "We might need a plan B." She makes a strange noise, and it takes me a second to realize she's *laughing*. Laughing—after we just drove a van into a mailbox.

And even though I'm scared and panicked and have no idea what to do next, I start laughing, too. I can't help it. The adrenaline spills out.

Reagan blinks at me, betrayal in her eyes. Then she hides her face in her hands, and I think she might cry—but then she's laughing, too. Sometimes it's the only thing to do.

"Does the van still work?" I ask once we can breathe again.

But Reagan doesn't have a chance to answer, because the lights in my parents' bedroom flick on. The front door flies open, and Mom comes running out of the house.

35

Mom never wastes time being surprised. As she always says, *Why react when you can act?*

And now, true to form, she runs toward us in her sweats, socks, and old T-shirt.

"*Mallory!*" she gasps as she yanks the van door open.

"Hello, Mrs. Moss," Reagan says. She's still gripping the steering wheel, but her voice is calm and even.

Mom stares at Reagan, then at Kath, then finally at me, eyes scanning for any visible injuries. "Out. All of you, out, now."

We file out and line up on the lawn, clasping our hands in front of us, digging our shoes into the grass.

"I don't even know where to start." Mom presses her fingertips together and closes her eyes, almost like she's praying, though I've never seen her pray before.

When she finally opens her eyes, she looks straight at me. "Explain."

I begin with the end. "We found Jennifer."

Mom freezes. For a moment, she lets herself feel surprise. And then, "Oh, Mallory. What did I say about this investigating? The police are still searching—"

"No," I interrupt. "We'rerunningoutoftimeandshe—"

"Mallory, slow down," Mom says.

Except there's no time to slow down. And then Reagan, Kath, and I are all talking at once.

I'm saying, "I wasn't trying to go behind your back, but I pieced everything together. And I had to make things right—"

And Kath is saying, "Ingrid and I were mad at Mallory, but when she figured out the code—"

And Reagan is saying, "I shouldn't have come. I shouldn't have gotten involved—"

Mom holds up a hand. "Girls, please. I can't follow when you're all talking over each other." Kneeling on the grass, so she's just a little shorter than me, she asks, "Mallory, why were you in that van?"

"We need to go to Howard Park," I tell her. "That's where Jennifer is."

Mom hesitates. "Why do you think that?"

"I don't think that. I know that. Well, I'm ninety-five percent sure I know that."

Mom pauses, debating. "I told you I need a reason to trust you."

My heart plummets. After our conversation this evening, I thought they were finally starting to understand me. But now I've blown it. "Sorry," I whisper.

Mom takes a deep breath. "But I didn't consider that

maybe *you* need a reason to trust *me*. You can always come to your dad and me. We're on your team. And if driving to Howard Park is what you need . . . I'll take you there."

I can see on her face that she doesn't believe Jennifer is there. But she believes I need this, and that's enough.

"Really?" My voice chokes with feeling.

"Really?" Kath asks. "You'll take us?"

Reagan stares at Mom the same way she always does, with a hard, angry jaw, and eyes that want to cry.

Mom stands back up and looks at my friends as if she forgot they were there. "Well . . . I can't take you all on a midnight road trip without your parents' permission." She sighs and rubs a hand over her face. "Come inside. I have to make some calls."

Reagan, Kath, and I sit on my bed as Mom calls their parents. We hear her in the other room, pacing back and forth, and we catch bits of her conversations: "They seem convinced"; "Wishful thinking, I'm sure, but maybe this is what they need"; and "Some kind of closure."

As we listen, Reagan tugs at her bangs and says, "What if you're wrong, Mal? What if this *is* just wishful thinking? What if Jennifer's . . . gone?"

Kath bites her nail. "Then we have to find out, don't we?"

Reagan doesn't respond.

"I'm positive Jennifer's at the park," I say. "She has to be."

"I don't think I—" Reagan stops. Collects herself. "Are you sure you want to see her?"

Though it's wrong, a part of me knows what she means. As much as I want to find Jennifer, there is a part of me that's afraid to face her.

"You can do this," Kath says gently.

I can't believe it took me so long to see the real Kath, the deep kindness beneath her prickly shield.

Before Reagan can respond, Mom and Dad walk into my bedroom. "Okay, Kath, I spoke to your parents," Mom says. "Your dad's coming to pick you up."

Kath looks at her hands. "Yes, Mrs. Moss."

Mom frowns. "And, Reagan, I can't get in touch with your dad. I assume he's asleep, so we can swing by your house and drop you off on our way."

"My dad's not home," Reagan says.

"What do you mean, he's not home?" The way Mom speaks to Reagan, it's almost like she's talking to another adult—an adult she doesn't really like.

Reagan shrugs. "He's on a business trip."

Dad blinks. "And you're home . . . alone?"

Reagan nods, like this is no big deal.

"How often does this happen?"

Reagan shrugs.

Mom and Dad exchange a look. They see the way Reagan's shoulders curl forward, like she's rolling in on herself. The way her left leg rattles with nerves. They see Reagan's unbrushed hair, her rubbed-raw eyes, the pimples dotting her chin, and the freckles sprinkling her cheeks. She looks younger without makeup.

Dad puts a hand on Mom's shoulder, and Mom's face softens. "Okay. Well. I guess you're coming with us."

Reagan's eyes widen and her freckles seem to glow. For a flash of a second, she smiles faintly, and then it's gone. She looks at the ground, her face unreadable again.

The moment is so shimmering-tense that when we hear a knock at the door, we all jump, expecting the police, or aliens, or even Jennifer herself.

We follow Mom into the living room, and when Mom opens the front door, there's Ingrid, twisting her hands in front of her.

"Ingrid," I blurt. "You came."

Her eyes flick between Reagan, my parents, Kath, and me. "There's a van in the middle of your lawn," she tells us, as if we might have missed that.

Kath nods gravely. "Indeed."

When nobody chooses to elaborate, Ingrid says, "I decided I should be with you two. I was still mad, but then I saw the crash outside, and I thought . . ." She winces. "But you're okay."

"We're okay," I confirm.

Mom turns to Dad, then Ingrid, and says, "Looks like I have another call to make."

36

The neighborhood is lit up. As we drive past, we see that nearly every house is decorated with strands of twinkling lights, though we're still months away from Christmas—and that's when I remember the news segment. Ms. Rodgers said she would light up her house, and now it seems other people have followed suit.

Looking out at this, something pinches behind my rib cage. I remember what Jennifer said that night in her tent: *If you could surround yourself with stars, why wouldn't you?*

Reagan said the hand-painted signs at school came from guilt, not care. But maybe it's both. Maybe people see, now, that they didn't do enough to welcome a new girl and her mom to the neighborhood. Maybe they know, now, that they should have ignored the rumors. They should have brought a pie.

They didn't then, but from now on, maybe we will do better.

And then the sky joins our sleepy little houses, lighting up with a show of its own. I press myself against the window, watching meteors streak through the night. We have to get to the park.

Mom spoke to Ingrid's mom, and they agreed that Ingrid could go with us, if this is what we needed for what they call *closure*. When Kath's dad got there, she convinced him to follow us in his car. So now it's Mom, Dad, Reagan, Ingrid, and me in our car—with Kath and her dad behind us.

Ingrid got into the car first, sitting where Reagan used to sit—and there was a moment of awkwardness before I slid into the middle seat. Normally, I would've felt uncomfortable sitting between Reagan and Ingrid, but right now I'm distracted.

"We're too late," I say, worried that we'll miss the meteor shower—and Jennifer along with it. "Drive. Please drive."

My parents do.

We dart through the night, chasing the stars. I barely breathe as we move through the outskirts of town, lined with car dealerships and thirsty palm trees—and then we're out of Norwell completely, surrounded by open fields.

A buzz rattles my bones, and I almost think it's aliens, shaking me out of my skin—but I realize it's just my phone, vibrating in my pocket.

What if we find Jennifer and she tells people what we did? It's Reagan texting. She's stiff, staring down at her phone.

Then we'll face it and learn to be better, I respond.

I watch her jaw tighten. She doesn't look like the Reagan I

249

used to know. She looks lost and scared. But now I think that behind those Shark Eyes, she's always been scared.

I don't know if I should be here, she writes. Followed by You don't need me anymore.

I think she means because I don't need a driver—but it kind of feels like more. I text, Don't you want to make this right?

If I'm not following, maybe I can lead. I can help her.

It won't matter anyway, she responds. When she finally meets my eyes, there's heartbreak on her face, and I know that even if she wants to fix this, she's not brave enough right now.

I set my phone down and give her a look that says *Thank you*. Thank you for trying. Thank you for being here now. Thank you for being who I needed, at one point in time.

But it also says *I'm sorry*. I'm sorry about your parents. I'm sorry about what we did. I'm sorry for the person I was, and maybe even the person I am. I'm sorry I can't be who you need anymore. And you can't be who I need, either.

I can say a lot without saying a word, but this feels like the end of our language. One day, maybe soon, Reagan and I won't understand each other anymore.

Swallowing, she nods, and her face says all of that back.

Why are people afraid to believe? Maybe it's because if they believe in a better world, then they have to work to make that world happen.

Reagan clicks her phone off and slides it between her knees. Then she stares out the window, watching the stars fall.

I turn to the map on my phone as we inch toward How-ard Park.

Seven more minutes.

When we finally get there, I throw the car door open before Mom even parks, and I'm sprinting, faster than I've ever run.

I am desperate. I am wild.

"Mallory!" Mom shouts. "Slow down."

But she's so far behind that I barely hear her.

Stars light the sky, and I'm running, calling Jennifer's name. As the field whips by, everything else seems to fade. The night seems too quiet, the air just a touch too cold. Every-thing feels like it's teetering on the edge of *happening*— and that's when I see her.

She's there—a small dot in the distance, at the base of the radio tower, starting to climb.

"Jennifer!" I cry. My lungs press against my beating heart, nearly suffocating, but I can't stop now.

It's not until I'm at the base of the tower that she looks down and sees me. She frowns, shaking her head like this doesn't compute.

"We found you!" I reach up, as if I could grab her and yank her down to safety. Her shoes are just above my fingertips. The laces of her left sneaker are untied. "We *found you*."

Jennifer loses her grip for a second, and my heart swoops, but she readjusts, tightening her hands into fists. *"Mallory?"*

she says. She looks past me and sees Reagan and Ingrid running toward her, sees my parents in the distance, and then Kath and her dad getting out of their car.

Her expression hardens from confusion to fear.

"I know you must have felt scared," I say. "But I'm here to tell you to come back. We shouldn't have said that stuff and taken those pictures and, well, the bathroom—you know. But we're sorry. It's okay now."

"You think it's *okay*?" she shouts, voice cracking on the last syllable. "God, why can't you just leave me alone?"

I blink, still out of breath from the run. "But—what?"

Her face twists with anger. "Why are you still doing this to me? Why are you always trying to pull me down?"

She climbs higher, and I watch her get farther away.

My ears buzz with nerves. And then all of a sudden I'm climbing, too. I hear my friends and parents screaming my name—but I keep going. The metal is so much colder than I imagined. It bites into my palms, and my hands shake.

"This is dangerous," I tell Jennifer, and as I say the words, they hit me. *Don't look down.* "You're scaring me."

Jennifer's laugh is harsh. "Do you know how much *you* scared *me*? Do you know how scared I was in that bathroom? Can you even understand?"

"Mal!" Mom pleads from beneath us, her voice unraveled, far more frantic than I've ever heard her. "Mallory! Jennifer! I'm calling the fire department. Please, girls, hold tight. Don't climb any further."

Jennifer climbs further.

So do I.

Hand over hand, foot over foot, I climb, with Jennifer always just out of reach. The wind stings my eyes with tears, but I don't dare wipe them away. The world goes water-blurred, and I almost lose my footing.

When Jennifer stops, we both pause on the tower, a moment to catch our runaway breath. She stares hard at her hands, and her words come out like a sob. "You wanted to make me disappear, to rip my life's work apart until I didn't know who I was anymore. You ripped *me* apart. You ripped me apart and you *laughed*."

"I didn't want to hurt you," I say.

"Then why did you?"

I should have considered my message. I should've planned what to say. Now I'm stumbling over my words. "I don't know. It wasn't . . . it wasn't personal."

Jennifer looks at the sky, at those stars burning the night. When she looks back down at me, her eyes are full of fire. "I spent so long trying to understand why you hurt me. I thought there was some big reason. I thought if I could just *understand* you, maybe it would all make sense. But . . . it wasn't personal." She laughs, cold and sharp as wind-kissed metal. "It wasn't *personal*. God, that's even worse."

"I'm sorry." I'm so quiet that I think the wind might have tossed my words away.

She doesn't say anything.

"I thought I saw aliens." Slowly, I climb up to reach her, until we're clinging to the tower side by side. "I saw a UAP.

For real this time. After you ran away, outside my room, I really saw one."

"I don't know," she says, and the fire in her eyes dims to ash. Her voice is flat, full of nothing. "I don't know why I ever believed in you, or in aliens, or in anything at all. They're not coming. No one's coming."

Her words hit me in the chest. I'm still out of breath from running and climbing, and when I look down, I immediately wish I didn't. The world seems to sway, like I'm rocking at the top of a Ferris wheel.

Everyone's gathered at the base of the tower, so small beneath us, and I hear them shouting, but I can't make out what they're saying beneath the raging wind.

I squeeze my aching fingers tighter and rip my eyes away from the ground, back to Jennifer.

"*I* came," I say.

She takes a shuddering breath. She looks to the stars. She does not look at me.

"I don't think I'll ever be able to explain why we did it," I say.

She turns to me, almost like she can't help it, and there's no hope on her face—but there's something almost close. "Try."

"I—I think there might be something bad in me," I confess. "This part of me that wants . . . more. I was afraid of it, and I thought I had to push it way down or else it would take over."

She swallows.

"I thought I had to make that feeling so small that it disappeared. But then I looked at you and you were . . . big. And you weren't afraid to be big and I just . . . I don't know why, but it made me mad. Because *I* wanted to feel that, for once, and I didn't know how. I still don't know how."

"So you tried to steal it from me."

"Maybe, so I could have it for myself. Or maybe I just didn't want you to have it."

She takes a deep breath.

"I'm sorry," I repeat.

Jennifer closes her eyes, and I look down. Below us, my friends and family shout and plead. My fingers hurt from clenching the bars. My vision pinpricks, and I expect to faint . . . but I don't.

Way up there, on the side of a radio tower, my Ferris wheel epiphany comes back to me. That night, I thought the world was fragile, that we couldn't live in it without knocking things down and hurting people.

But maybe there's more to it. Like, if we knock things down, maybe we can rebuild them. If we hurt, maybe we can help.

And I don't know if it's the adrenaline or something more, but I'm not as afraid as I usually am. I'm still scared, of course, but I know we're going to be all right. We're going to climb down, and everything is going to be all right.

In the distance, I hear sirens. "Please," I say. "Come down."

She hesitates and shifts, releasing her grip just slightly. A knot unspools in my chest. We're going to be all right.

Then the sky flashes, lightning bright. Everything goes white.

And Jennifer Chan loses her grip.

I scream, reaching out to grab her—but it's too late.

Jennifer Chan is falling.

There are some moments that make you believe. Moments that are so strange, so impossible, that they imprint on your memory forever. They change who you are and make you believe in something bigger.

Because Jennifer is falling, and then, just as quickly, she isn't.

Time stops.

Years into the future, the details will grow fuzzy, and I'll look back on this and wonder if I really saw anything at all.

But right now I'm here: halfway up a radio tower, clinging to its side, staring at a girl who is not quite falling.

The flash of light narrows to a single beam, and Jennifer is illuminated, suspended inside it.

Everything slow-motions except for the meteors, scraps of stars streaking through the sky above us. Jennifer and I lock eyes, and her expression mirrors my own emotions—frightened, panicked, and a tiny bit hopeful.

Is it possible? Could it be?

The light blinks once, twice, three times, and her eyes grow wider. Wisps of her hair float above her shoulders, and it's like she's held by an invisible, unknowable force, a force even stronger than gravity.

I wonder what, exactly, is happening and what, exactly, I'm supposed to believe in.

And then the moment stretches and snaps. Time restarts.

Jennifer is falling.

And I am afraid.

((((((38))))))

The days following seem to blur and drag, expand and contract, all at the same time.

A fire truck got to Howard Park just minutes after Jennifer fell, and the paramedics rushed her to the ER. Thankfully, she was okay aside from a broken leg, and now she's taking some time off from school to recover at home.

My parents have let me take a few days off, too, and I spend them alternating between worry and relief. Dad has fed me so much sauerkraut that I'm honestly pretty sick of it.

Five days after the fall, Kath and Ingrid knock on my door.

Jennifer hasn't wanted to see me, so Kath and Ingrid have been coming over to give me updates after visiting her. They've returned Jennifer's journals and made their own amends with her, and from them, I've learned that she spent the first night hiding in the mall bathroom, and the last few camping in the woods, sending signals to the sky with a tinkered-up radio she made with her dad. One of those signals interfered, briefly, with the local station's signal while we were driving with Mom. At the radio station, Kath, Ingrid, and I intercepted another, her Morse code message about where she'd be.

Today I ask Kath and Ingrid how Jennifer's recovering, and Ingrid launches into an explanation of all the research she's been doing on bone fractures. Kath and I listen, soaking in all those facts, and when she's finished, Kath says, "Jennifer's ready to talk to you."

I sit up straighter. "Really?" I've been wanting to talk to Jennifer all week, but suddenly I'm scared. I don't want to mess this up again.

Ingrid gives me a soft smile, and Kath reaches over to squeeze my arm. Kath, Ingrid, and I aren't back to where we were before, but after our night in Howard Park, we can't deny it: we're bonded over something bigger. They've decided to look forward instead of back, and we're working to become the people we believe we can be.

After they leave, I put a slice of Mom's pie on our very best plate. Then I grab my gift for Jennifer and walk across the street.

"This is for you," I say, holding out the pie as soon as Ms. Chan opens the front door. Mom's already been over, of course. She's been baking a lot of pies lately.

Rebecca Chan eyes the plate warily. She's not exactly my biggest fan, and after everything that's happened, I don't blame her. But eventually she takes it and gestures for me to come inside.

"How did you . . ." She hesitates. "How did you know where she was?"

"Um." I feel like there's a bigger question hiding beneath her smaller one. "She gave me one of her journals. The answer was in there."

She closes her eyes. "It should have been me," she says, and I think she's speaking to herself more than to me. "I should've figured it out."

When she opens her eyes again, she adds, "Be kind to her. She deserves kindness."

"I know." I can't quite express how much I've learned that.

She takes me to her daughter's room, and after she closes the door, I can feel her waiting just outside.

Jennifer's room is stuffed full of flowers and chocolate, and the heady scent fills my eyes with unexpected tears. I blink them away. So many of our classmates have sent something. I even spot sunflowers from Reagan and a teddy bear from Pete.

"Hi," Jennifer says. She's lying in bed, bruised, with her leg propped up in a cast, but she looks better than I expected. Though I've already heard as much from Kath and Ingrid, I feel my shoulders relax.

"Hi," I respond, taking careful steps toward her. "I brought you something."

I fumble with my backpack zipper, feeling clumsier than I ever have, and after what seems like an hour, I manage to pull out a brand-new notebook. "Volume Eight," I offer. "If you want it."

She takes a breath as I set it on the table next to her, but she says nothing.

"Are you . . . um . . . how are you?" I ask.

"Sore," she says.

"I'm sorry."

"When you all said you wanted to bring me back to Earth, I didn't think you meant it literally."

Her joke startles a laugh out of me, and then I feel bad, because I'm not sure if I'm allowed to laugh yet.

But her lips lift a bit. "The local news wants to do an interview with me."

I nod. "They asked Kath, Ingrid, and me, too, but we told them they should talk to you first. It's your story."

"True." She considers this. "But it's your story, too."

I didn't really think about it like that, and I'm surprised she does. "As the bad guy?" I ask. "As the reason you ran?"

"Don't give yourself so much credit." She smiles, and I smile back, and it feels good. Then she gets serious. "As one of the reasons, yes. But not fully. I wanted to prove something. I wanted to find an actual answer out there."

"I don't know if there's an answer out there," I say. "But maybe there's one here, on Earth. With us."

She looks at me. Then she laughs. "That's cheesy, Mallory. Have you always been so cheesy?"

I've never thought of myself like that, but it doesn't seem so bad. "Maybe."

"Kath and Ingrid told me what you did while I was gone, how you all looked for me," she says. "And I don't know if what happened in the bathroom can be undone, but . . . thank you. For finding me."

"Thank *you*," I say. "You showed me how to believe."

Her eyes dart away from mine, and she's suddenly too emotional to speak.

"I was so scared when you fell," I blurt. "I didn't know if you'd be okay."

"I'm surprised I was," she whispers. "We were up so high and there was this flash of lightning and I . . . It was like . . . I felt . . ." She trails off, uncertain.

I don't know if this is what she was going to say, but I lean forward and confess, "It looked like you were floating."

Her eyes widen. "That's exactly what it felt like. But when I asked Kath and Ingrid, they said it happened quickly. They just saw me fall."

I shake my head. "They said that when I asked, too, but I saw you. You froze."

"And that lightning came out of nowhere."

I nod. "We get a lot of lightning in Florida, but not like *that*. That felt like something more."

We stare at each other, and for a moment, everything else washes away. We're two people who saw something impossible. But we don't say what we're really thinking, what we believe or hope it might have been.

Maybe one day we'll talk more—maybe we'll investigate everything in the last few days that can't be explained. Maybe we'll consider the UAP I saw in the sky, and whether it could have been aliens, or something from the military base, or a god, or just the almost magic you see when you desperately want to believe.

One day we might bond over our questions, sealing over

the deep canyon cracks between us, bringing us toward some-thing like friendship.

Maybe.

"Should we tell the reporters?" I ask. "About the unex-plainable stuff?"

She raises a brow. "It might make this town like Area 51. It could turn Norwell into somewhere special."

I consider this, what it would be like if Nowhereville were actually Somewhereville. But then I think about the search party, and the handmade signs, and all those houses lit up with twinkling hope. "Maybe it already is," I tell her. "Or at least, I think it can be, if people keep caring. Even without aliens."

"That's nice." She looks at me like she's seeing something new, or something different. And at first, I feel that old flash of worry—that need to know what she's thinking. Then it fades, as quickly as it came.

"Do you want to know my favorite space fact?" she asks.

"Oh," I say, surprised she wants to share it with me. "Yes, okay."

"Don't worry," she adds with an almost smile. "It's not about aliens."

"I wasn't worried."

She nods. "My favorite fact is that all the hydrogen in the universe was created during the big bang. And the human body is ten percent hydrogen. Which means ten percent of us is as old as the universe itself."

I try to wrap my brain around that. A week ago, the

thought might have made me dizzy, but now I mean it when I say, "That's really cool."

"It makes the universe feel a little more connected. Like, even if aliens don't exist, even if we're all alone, we aren't *really* alone, because we're all made of the same stuff. We always have been, since the very beginning. Do you know what I mean?"

The world feels out of proportion. Something grows in my chest, and at first it feels like that familiar anxiety. But it's not—it's something bigger, and more hopeful, like an infinite expanse of possibility. "Yeah," I tell her. "I think I kinda do."

Jennifer Chan's Guide to the Universe
Volume VIII, Entry No. 1: Who Do You Think You Are?

The beginning of everything started with a bang.

Everything was silent until <u>bang</u>, all that mess and light and life. There was no way back. Nothing could stuff all that messiness back into a tiny speck of dust.

It's only getting bigger, you know—the universe. And in all that infinite space, there's so much out there to learn and discover. There's so much out there that we don't understand.

I'm still searching for answers, of course, because that's who I am. But after falling from that tower—after <u>not falling</u> from that tower—I thought . . . maybe the invisible, mysterious stuff isn't so scary after all.

Ten percent of the universe is known. But ninety percent is waiting for discovery.

Ten percent of us is made from the oldest element in the universe. And ninety percent of us is new.

So maybe the parts of us that we don't understand aren't good or bad, but somewhere in between, somewhere that can be anything.

A fact about the universe: nobody knows how it's going to end. Some scientists predict a Big Crunch, gravity pulling everything in until it all implodes. Others think it'll be a Big

Rip, dark energy growing so strong it tears everything apart. And others think it'll keep on going like it currently is, a universe running from itself forever.

But as long as it's impossible to know, I may as well have a theory.

Scientists talk about gravity and dark energy as if they're in a tug-of-war. But I don't think it's a battle at all. I think these forces were always meant to work together—not to create the end of everything, a Big Crunch or a Big Rip, but to maintain an ebb and flow. Expansion and contraction.

We push each other away. We pull each other close.

We hurt each other. Then we help.

We explore the vastness of the cosmos. And we come back home.

The push and pull of forces within us inspire us to change and discover. And I think it's good, at least that's what I choose to believe, because we're all so much bigger than we know. We're all part of this vast universe, full of infinite, messy life.

Author's Note

I was the girl in the bathroom—the girl pressed up against the sinks, surrounded by a group of my classmates. Some of the girls I'd been friends with, others I'd thought I was *still* friends with, and others I'd never spoken to before.

The bullying had started on social media when I was in middle school. At twelve, they'd written messages to and about me that were too violent to include in a novel for twelve-year-olds. They'd made plans to spike my drinks, break me, drown me.

I told myself and others I wasn't scared. During the day, I tried to act like none of it bothered me. But I spent sleepless nights hiding under my covers, waiting for it to end.

After a couple of weeks of rapid escalation, the bullying moved from online to in person, and they cornered me in a bathroom on the last day of school.

I want to make this the worst day of your sad little life, one of them said. *I hope you always remember it.*

And I do.

I remember the crack in the bathroom wall, the flickering of the dim fluorescent light, the way one of them looked at me and said, *Who do you think you are?*

They told me I was nothing, that I would always be nothing.

I remember thinking, *Don't cry, don't cry,* until they finally left and I curled up in a stall and sobbed on the cold, grimy tile, wondering if they were right.

It felt like the end of everything.

When I told my teachers, they said there was nothing they could do; no adults had witnessed the bullying, and the school year was ending anyway. *Enjoy the summer,* they said. *You'll forget about this before you know it.*

Not knowing where else to turn, I wrote about the Incident in my journal, as if to tell myself, *This happened. This mattered.*

I invented thinly veiled fiction about bullying in that journal, writing as if I could excavate my experience for explanations. *Where had I gone wrong? Why were those girls so mad at me? What made them want to hurt me?* I imagined answers for myself, hoping that would help me understand.

It helped a little, as writing often does, but I felt like I was missing something, like I couldn't find the right answers or I wasn't asking the right questions. Eventually I told myself to move on. I tried to forget about the Incident.

And that worked, kind of. We can become numb to our memories the same way we become numb to the scent of our homes—steeped in it so often, we forget there's any scent at all. I stopped noticing my long-buried pain.

And then I started writing books about middle school.

I dug up old experiences as I visited schools, as I spoke with current students and shared my stories and listened to theirs. It was like coming home after a long journey and realizing, *My goodness, my house smells like lemon peels!*

I'd spent so long running from that moment in the bathroom that I felt disoriented returning to it. But students kept asking about my middle school experience, and when I told them I'd been bullied, they had so many questions.

What did you say? Why did it happen? How did you deal with it?

I found myself giving versions of the advice I'd heard from adults: *You'll be okay. One day you'll forget all about this.*

But my words rang hollow. Those students wanted answers, just as I had at twelve—just as I still did. And while speaking to them in those middle school auditoriums and classrooms, I was revisiting the girl I'd been. I realized I needed to tell her story. I owed that to the kids who were asking questions, and I owed it to myself, too.

A friend was puzzled when I told them about my latest writing project. *Why would you return to that memory and hurt yourself all over again?*

I didn't have much of an answer yet except to say, *I think I have to.*

My first drafts of *Jennifer Chan* were similar to my middle school journal entries, all those years ago. After trying for so long to forget, I started by telling myself, *This happened. This mattered.*

In those early versions, I was seeking answers—and I figured that as an adult, I was finally brave enough to go to the source.

I reached out to my former bullies.

We met for coffee, or messaged, or spoke on Zoom, and I asked what had made them hurt me.

Not all of those conversations were easy. There were some people who wouldn't acknowledge what had happened—who'd forgotten, or refused to remember.

But some remembered, or refused to forget, and they asked, *What do you want to know? I'll do my best.*

Fifteen years after the Incident, I was suddenly twelve again, heart pounding, palms sweating, seeking an answer that would make sense of the world.

Why me? I asked.

They did their best. But the best they could offer was *It wasn't personal.*

And to be honest, that wasn't the response I was looking for. After all, it was so very personal to me. If I could have been anybody—if I'd just happened to be in the wrong place, with the wrong people, at the wrong time—then it was as if I didn't matter in my own story.

But of course, this wasn't only my story; it was theirs, too. And their answer was an invitation, in a way, because if this wasn't personal, what was?

I realized I'd been asking the wrong questions. I'd been focused on one moment in time: *Why did you say those things about me? Why did you do those things to me?* But I needed to go broader, gentler: *Who were you? Who did you want to become? Who have you become?*

Put simply, I found myself asking the same question my bullies had once asked me: *Who do you think you are?*

I'd been running from the question for fifteen years. In their mouths, those words had been a challenge, an accusation, a reminder not to reach so high.

But as an adult, looking back on the past and forward to the future, I saw that the question could be bigger than that.

I'd wanted to know, *What makes a bully?* But I should have been asking, *What makes a person?*

It's a question without an answer. Or rather, it's a question with infinite answers.

The conversations shifted, and we talked about who we were in middle school, about our home lives and school lives, about our dreams and insecurities. My former bullies told me that they'd learned, that they'd grown. One of them confessed that she'd been angry, hurting in a way that no adult could really see, and there'd been nowhere else for her anger to go. Another told me that she herself had felt so small.

One of them shared the ways that hurting me—and hurting others—had changed her, how her actions had become a mirror that pushed her to do better and be better. Another is an activist now, trying to make the world a gentler place for kids today.

In these conversations, we navigated our way backward from adulthood to adolescence, forging a path into one moment in time. It wasn't easy to return. But by finding a way in, we also found a way back out. And I realized that I wasn't hurting myself all over again. Instead, I was healing, truly, for the first time.

Healing came first from acknowledging that this trauma had happened. It had hurt me. It had scared me. It had shattered my belief that the world was safe and simple. But it had also taught me to rebuild, to stand up for others, to see myself as resilient. Healing came from understanding that this experience mattered, that *I* mattered.

And healing came from recognizing that I am not locked in that one moment—and neither are my bullies. Healing was seeing the messiness in others and in myself. It was learning to forgive. It was realizing that change is not a given—but it is possible.

When I was twelve, afraid of my bullies and too scared to go to school, the advice adults gave me was *You'll be okay. One day you'll forget all about this.*

The first part was true. The second part wasn't.

And I still don't have answers to all the questions students ask me. But to those kids, I'll say this:

If you are being bullied, if you know someone who's being bullied, or if you've hurt someone—know that one day you will be okay. This is not the end of everything.

And maybe one day you *will* forget this experience.

But that is not my wish for you. My wish for you is that one day you will heal from it and grow from it.

I wish that one day you will see your experiences not as an end but as a beginning—the beginning of knowing yourself as someone who forges pathways and fosters empathy, someone who believes in goodness and possibility, someone who sees, even in the darkest nights, an infinite expanse of stars.

I hope that day comes soon.

In the meantime, tell a parent, teacher, or trusted loved one. Find safe spaces in your school, in your home, in your heart. And know that you matter. Know that you are not alone.

Acknowledgments

Caroline Abbey: Thank you for believing in this book from the very start and for geeking out in all aspects of this story, from the space facts, to the psychological impacts of shame, to the very middle school experience of wearing makeup for the first time. I am so grateful for your guidance throughout the whole writing process.

And I am hugely grateful to the team at Random House: Barbara Marcus, Judith Haut, Michelle Nagler, Mallory Loehr, Barbara Bakowski, Katharine Wiencke, Katrina Damkoehler, Jasmine Hodge, Kelly McGauley, Adrienne Waintraub, Kristin Schulz, Kris Kam, John Adamo, Emily DuVal, Erica Stone, Shaughnessy Miller, Laura Hernandez, Emily Bruce, and more.

Thank you also to Dion MBD for the excellent cover art.

Sarah Davies and Chelsea Eberly: Thank you for supporting me through the writing of this book.

And Faye Bender: Thank you for taking it across the finish line.

A big thank-you to my incredible writing and publishing friends, who keep me sane in this roller coaster of an industry: Lauren Magaziner, Booki Vivat, Sam Morgan, Aly Gerber, Bree Barton, Lauren Grange, and Ben Grange. What would I do without your business advice, storytelling genius, text threads, and emails?

I also drew on the knowledge of experts for this book. Thank you to Matt Granato for explaining how radios work and guiding my story into (or at least *near*) the realm of possibility. Thank you also to the officers at the Tukwila Police Department for informing me about police protocols. And though I didn't speak to them, thank you to Carl Sagan, Neil deGrasse Tyson, Sarah Scoles, and Evalyn Gates for writing books that were essential in my astrophysics and alien research. My gratitude as well to some former classmates who offered their insights, perspectives, and reflections when I messaged them out of the blue: "Hey, can we talk about the people we used to be?"

Mom and Dad: Have I ever properly thanked you for all your support through those middle school years? I was in so much pain at school, but you gave me such a safe place at home, and I didn't realize how important that was until years later. Thank you.

Sunhi: Thank you for inspiring me to be brave. You always have.

And to all my sibs, Sunhi, Emily, and Henry: The single silver lining of the pandemic was spending so much time with you. Thank you for all the big conversations about kindness, cruelty, and the state of the world. Your wisdom has certainly made its way into this book, probably more than you know.

Of course, Josh: I feel lucky every day I'm with you. Thank you for being the best chef, best listener, best podcast cohost, best friend, and absolute best person to spend a life with. Thank you also for the title of this book.

And last, but very far from least: I started this book in

February 2020, a month before the United States shut down. It was not an easy time to write a novel, but it certainly put my small-potatoes writerly angst in perspective. So I want to express my enormous gratitude for health care professionals, grocery store employees, scientists, and all essential workers. A huge thank-you, too, to the many people who have done their best to keep themselves and others safe and have responded to all this grief and uncertainty with empathy and compassion. Seeing what others have done for their communities and for strangers has given me a great deal of comfort and hope. It has reminded me that even in the worst of times, people can be good.

About the Author

TAE KELLER is the Newbery Award–winning and *New York Times* bestselling author of *When You Trap a Tiger* and *The Science of Breakable Things*. She was born and raised in Honolulu and now lives in Seattle with her husband and a mountain of books. She hasn't seen a UAP . . . yet. Follow her monthly love letters at bit.ly/lovetae.

TaeKeller.com